FROM ERIK'S DIARY
(LORELAI AND I)

EPISODE 5

THE SCARLET
TELEPHONE

Massimo Indrio

© Massimo Indrio
www.massimoindrio.com
first edition: August 2015
ISBN: 978-88-940304-7-1
Translation by Brett Auerbach-Lynn

CHAPTER 1

It had been at least twenty years since the scarlet telephone, the one in the forbidden closet, had shown any signs of life, but I remembered the sound of it quite well even though I'd heard it only once. My uncle Archibald had locked it away so that he would never again have to hear its unpleasant sound, which closely resembled the squawk of a particularly tone-deaf crow.

I call it "scarlet," but in truth only the oval scale-covered base of the phone was that color. The bat wing-shaped receiver and the rotating disc were black as night. And the numbers, which weren't actually numbers but incomprehensible symbols, were made of gold. So were the three owl's feet on which the apparatus perched.

Uncle Archibald had purchased it at an auction, paying an outrageous price against the express wishes of his wife Evelyn.

I remembered that telephone quite clearly although I hadn't seen it since I was little more than a child. I also remembered the day I'd seen it for the last time, for that was precisely the day Aunt Evelyn vanished into thin air.

My uncle blamed her disappearance on the telephone because, all of a sudden, despite not being plugged-in, it began to ring with that awful sound. It croaked five or six times and then went silent. No one had had the courage to pick up, although I really wanted to. Afterwards Aunt Evelyn disappeared. My uncle immediately assumed it was due to supernatural causes, but I suspected that she had left of her own free will, enraged by his rash purchase.

From that moment sprung a whole series of unfortunate events: Uncle Archibald's deep depression, the distressing apparitions of the ghost of Duke Siegfried, the sudden collapse of the north wing of the palace, the annoying hiccups of the cook, Josephine, my uncle's decision to depart for the Gobi Desert and, finally, the auctioning off of my beloved collection of figurines. All these mishaps marked me indelibly and helped make me the man I am today. This sequence of painful events hit me pretty hard at the time, but gradually I found the strength to fight back and came away all the stronger for it. Undoubtedly I owe my now habitual nonchalance and stoicism to this. Yet for many long years I despised that infernal apparatus which I too unconsciously blamed for everything that had happened. That is why it didn't exactly make me jump for joy to suddenly hear that unpleasant sound after so long.

I hesitated to answer, so after five or six caws the telephone went silent. Lorelai stuck her head in the doorway and asked, "What was that horrible noise? It sounded like somebody sawing a plastic tube in slow-motion."

I personally found the comparison with a tone-deaf crow to be both more exact and less bizarre, but I decided not to waste time arguing and answered, "It was the telephone."

"The telephone? What are you talking about? How could it be the telephone? The telephone? But our telephone has Beethoven's Ninth as its ringtone!"

"Not the normal telephone, the scarlet one in the forbidden closet," I clarified.

"We have another telephone? You mean another telephone line? Why don't I know anything about this? And where are the bills for this *other* telephone? Why does it make that horrible noise? Why haven't you ever let me into this 'forbidden' closet? Who the heck are you – Blue Beard?"

Here was Lorelai's typical burst of questions. It was very difficult to answer them because by the time she'd gotten to the last one you'd already forgotten the first, but I did my best. "I'm not Blue Beard, the forbidden closet's not really 'forbidden' but there are things in there that are better to stay away from, I don't know why it makes that awful sound, there have never been any bills because the telephone's not plugged in, and also because it comes directly from the tomb of Assurbanipal, king of Babylon."

I actually remember hearing Uncle Archibald reveal this last detail in his final heated argument with his wife, attempting to justify the exorbitant price he'd paid.

Just as my aunt had done back then, Lorelai made an acute observation. "But there were no telephones back in those days!"

Besides the absence of the final epithet "moron," this was exactly the same response that Aunt Evelyn had given to my uncle.

When he had replied, "Don't you understand? That's exactly what makes it a unique object of inestimable value!" my aunt let out a shriek, fell silent, made an about-turn and left the room, just as the telephone began to croak for no apparent reason.

She was never seen again.

I decided not to repeat Uncle Archibald's response to Lorelai, reasoning that its logic wasn't exactly air-tight, and thus voiced my agreement with her, saying, "It seems strange to me too. Just like it seems strange that it's just rung again after twenty years of silence."

"It hasn't rung for twenty years?"

"Nope."

Lorelai frowned, raising her eyes to the ceiling and plunging her long fingers into her bushy mane of soft blonde hair to scratch her head, and then after thinking it over, she said,

"Listen, my mysterious little sweetie pie, why don't we go inside and take a look?"

CHAPTER 2

I hadn't stepped foot in that closet for so long that I didn't even remember what was in there anymore. Over the years I'd heard strange legends about that little room, some of which were so improbable that I'd never given them much credence. For example, I'd heard that whoever passed through that door came down with an incurable fever, thanks to the curse of Pharaoh Aspirin I, brother of Achenhotep III, but this had always seemed a bit over the top to me. Some said that my great-great-great-great grandmother, Lucille the Lunatic, had met her grandfather's father's son in that closet and then lost her mind. Put this way, such a revelation can be quite shocking. But when you think about it for a minute, you realize that no one has ever lost their mind just by meeting their own grandfather in a closet.

These tall tales aside, the truth was that for generations members of my family had stuck in that closet every strange, mysterious and - most of all - potentially dangerous object that they had accumulated. I myself had used it to store two or three things of the sort: the rotating reaping-hook of the wizard Melchior, the self-strangulating rope of the necromancer Bogus, and a CD of hypno-subjugating music that came from a tribe of cannibals in Kurumbo Matango.

So I had a few of my own good reasons for not wanting to open that door, but upon reflection I made up my mind to go in. I figured that there must have been a good reason for the telephone to come back to life and I intended to find out what it was. I did however take some precautions. To make a long story short, I grabbed my trusty carbon-reinforced, double oblong-barreled Fergusson K-16 pistol and, gripping it tightly, approached the closet's old but stout little door.

First I took down the sign reading "Abandon all hope, he who enters here" that my uncle had hung on it since it seemed a slight exaggeration, and then I inserted the large key into the keyhole and unlocked the door.

"How exciting!" exclaimed Lorelai, looking on from behind me. "I can't wait to have a look at all these strange things."

I turned around and looked straight into her blue eyes. By my concerned expression she knew she'd said something wrong.

"But my grumpy little sweetie-pie ..." she whimpered, but she couldn't finish because I silenced her with a kiss on the mouth, swallowing half a kilo of lipstick in the process. Then I said to her, "You know Lorelai, I'd really hate to lose you."

"What do you mean?"

"That if you value your life you'd better not touch anything."

She smiled and replied, "I promise," but I'd be willing to wager dinner at Peppino Mastrocece's restaurant that the clever girl had a hand hidden behind her back with two fingers crossed.

"Stay behind me," I told her, "and don't be frightened by the first thing you see." In fact, no sooner had I opened the door than we heard a terrifying roar and saw an enormous lion emerge out of the darkness and lunge directly at us with claws bared and jaws wide open.

Lorelai screamed and cowered behind me, but just as a dream dissolves upon waking, the lion disappeared as soon as it reached the doorway.

"This time it was a lion, last time it was a dragon, and the time before that a harpy," I explained to her. "They're merely images produced by the cylinder of Ollatrep, a generator of three-dimensional holograms that's activated automatically when the door opens. Uncle Archibald made sure to place it there to guard the closet and discourage visitors."

"Great idea!" Lorelai commented as she got her breath and color back. "A really wonderful idea! It nearly killed me!"

"Yeah, you're right, my uncle really did have a tendency to go overboard."

"I'm not mad at him! I'm mad at *you* for not warning me."

"But I did warn you!"

"Oh shut up!"

I decided to let it go and, after turning on the light, stepped into the closet. I didn't remember it being so crammed full of ... things. There was a large wardrobe at least two centuries old, an Egyptian sarcophagus complete with mummy, a great antique table cluttered with boxes, cases, trunks, bags, guns and daggers, and then everywhere crates, bags, strongboxes, swords, scimitars, halberds and a lot of other stuff not easy to identify. As I'd expected, Lorelai passed right by me and went in first, clapping her hands and exclaiming, "Amazing! So many fascinating things!" But when she clapped her hands three times, the mummy suddenly arose from the sarcophagus and grabbed her by the neck. It thrashed the rash young lady from side to side, her tongue hanging out of her mouth. Things would certainly have ended very badly if I hadn't grabbed a large scimitar and cut the head clean off of that embalmed assassin come back to life.

Lorelai collapsed into a large stuffed chair that was strangely devoid of objects. Massaging her throat, she said "Gosh, sweetie pie, who could've expected that? I didn't touch a thing."

"I know, but in here you have to expect the unexpected."

"Oh Mama, oh Mama," she said, continuing to massage her neck. "Maybe it's better if I wait for you outside."

"That sounds like a good idea."

Before leaving, however, she cast a glance at the large wardrobe in front of her and asked innocently, "What's the meaning of the inscription up there: '*Extra habitas inferus malum*?'"

As soon as these words left her mouth, the doors of the wardrobe swung open. A chasm opened up inside it, emitting flames, smoke, and an infernal shrieking. Then a swarm of giant bats surged out, and we heard a terrifying voice saying, "Who dares utter the cursed phrase after four thousand years!"

"Quick, Lorelai!" I shouted, "Let's get out of here!"

We were barely able to throw ourselves out of the closet. As I kicked the door closed behind me, we heard a roar from within and then a series of crashes which gradually diminished in intensity until they ceased completely. Apparently that little door was not only quite strong but also made from the wood of a magic tree.

Lorelai got up, dusted herself off, and then said in her defense, "You told me not to touch anything and I didn't touch anything, but how was I supposed to know that I couldn't talk either?"

"I know that's something that's particularly difficult for you," I replied, trying my best to be understanding.

"What are we going to do now about the telephone? Wild horses couldn't drag me back in there."

"That won't be necessary," I said, showing her the scarlet telephone that I'd grabbed just before launching myself out the door."

CHAPTER 3

"Well done, sugar plum!" Lorelai exclaimed, throwing her arms around me. "I don't know how you did it, but you did great!"

"Then I deserve a reward, don't you think?" I asked her as we headed towards the yellow parlor.

"I certainly think so. Your wish is my command," she replied, with a mischievous smile that made it seem as if she expected who knows what response from me, but I said to her very simply, "Good, then please don't call me 'sugar plum' anymore."

"If that's all you want," she answered a bit resentfully, "then don't worry, it won't be a problem." But she was immediately distracted by the telephone. I had placed it on the large walnut table, and she exclaimed, "It's gorgeous!"

And indeed it was. Strangely, it was dust-free despite all the years it had been in the closet. It occurred to me that the dust might have been repelled by an energy field emitted by the apparatus itself.

The red scales that covered it shone iridescently and the engraved receiver and the disc with white symbols in place of numbers were so intensely black that they seemed to absorb all the light around them.

"I wonder when it's going to ring again," said Lorelai, sitting down sadly and propping herself up on her elbows.

No sooner had she spoken than our ears were once again assaulted by the horrendous croaking that that strange apparatus used, however rarely, to express itself. I went to answer, but Lorelai beat me to it.

"Hello?" she chirped. "Yes? Who? No. That's okay, don't worry about it. See you soon" and hung up. Then, turning to me, she giggled and said, "How silly, I said 'see you soon,' but on the phone it would be better to say 'talk to you soon.'"

"Who on earth was it!?!?" I yelled, flabbergasted that she had hung up.

"Oh, nobody. It was a wrong number."

"What do you mean it was a wrong number!!?" I bellowed. "Can't you see that this phone isn't plugged in? Didn't you think to ask who it was and where they were calling from?"

"Golly, calm down, my furious little sparrow. My cell phone isn't plugged in and it still works! And anyway, I simply didn't think of it, so there's really no cause to get so upset."

She was right; there was no reason to get

so angry. I took a deep breath and asked her, "What kind of voice was it? Was it a man or a woman? Who were they looking for?"

"It was a man, and he was looking for a certain Monique Lefruit. Who knows, maybe he thought he was calling France."

I was startled to hear this name. Sometime before this, during an auto-hypnotic regression to previous lives, I remembered that I had once been a charming French spy named Monique Lefruit. During World War II, Lefruit was able to infiltrate Adolf Hitler's entourage and got within a whisker of killing him.

Lorelai put her arms around me, kissed me and said, "Sorry, sugar plum. You're right. I shouldn't have hung up so quickly. Next time, you answer." Despite the fact that she'd once again called me "sugar plum," peace was restored. I could never stay angry at her for more than ten seconds.

"I wonder when it'll ring again," she said. "The last time it was silent for twenty years."

"The second-to-last time," I corrected her.

"Before it rang just now, I was thinking about opening it up to see how it's made," she said, lifting up the apparatus to look underneath and see if there were any screws.

But there were no screws. So I laid it down on the table and picked up the receiver, bringing it to my ear. Silence. Then, just as I was about to put it down again, there was the faintest sound. I motioned to Lorelai to be quiet and listened attentively. What I heard was a very soft music, like a chorus of a thousand voices that seemed to come from very far away.

"I hear music," I told Lorelai.

"They must have put you on hold," she said. "But I'm getting hungry. I'll go to the kitchen to see if I can find something to munch on. Are there any Hungarian cookies left?" Having said this, she walked out and I was left alone with the strange contraption.

CHAPTER 4

With my ear to the receiver, I continued listening to that celestial music which had me completely in raptures. However it was suddenly interrupted by a male voice that asked me, "Is Monique Lefruit there?"

"Yes, that's me," I answered instinctively, but then I corrected myself. "Well, I mean that *was* me."

"Yes, I know, there's no need to explain. I'm calling you from the Corrections Office. We know that you have somehow been able to recall your previous life. If you hadn't done so, we wouldn't be disturbing you. In that life a tiny mistake was made and, if you agree, we would like to send you back to correct it."

I wasn't sure if I understood, so I asked, "What mistake? And by whom?"

"You certainly remember, Monique, dying in Berlin in the arms of your lover, Lieutenant Gert Von Krapfen, on a rainy autumn evening after being hit by a bus."

"Yes, I remember it well."

"Well, things weren't really supposed to go like that. Monique was supposed to dodge the bus, survive and successfully conclude her mission."

"You mean kill Hitler?"

"Precisely."

"And you call that a 'tiny' mistake?!"

"An unforgiveable error, I know, but which was then remedied by other means."

"But how could it have happened?"

"The technicians who weave the wefts of destiny had some problems. Several strings got tangled up and the outcome was difficult to unravel. As I've told you, the error was corrected, but the great tapestry of creation now has a very noticeable mend at that juncture that's not pleasant to look at. If you're willing to co-operate, everything could fall perfectly back into place."

"Go back to wartime just to fix a mend? No thanks," I replied firmly. "I'm a sucker for aesthetics myself, but it seems to me that the game in this case isn't worth the candle. Plus, I imagine that by changing the past I'd change the present as well, and thus my current life would also be modified. Meaning that I wouldn't have attended the esoteric school on Mount Arius, I wouldn't have participated in the rediscovery of the ancient city of Shangri-La, I wouldn't have met Lorelai, I wouldn't have won the "Noah's Ark" prize, and so on and so forth."

"You've got it all wrong. As I've just told you, a mend has been made such that from that point on, everything has gone smoothly, just as it should have. Look, I'll give you two good reasons to accept: the first is that you might discover something very interesting, something you didn't have time to discover during your hypnotic regression."

"About what?"

"It would be more correct to say about whom."

"About Lieutenant Gert Von Krapfen! He was Lorelai!" I burst out.

"Who told you? That's classified information!"

"My sixth and seventh sense, I think. I have to admit that this news really is very interesting."

"Damn, it wasn't part of the plan for you to know this from the start."

"Well, it doesn't seem to me to be too serious a breach. But why don't you give me the second reason."

"The second reason is that our Superior, who is also yours and everyone else's, would be infinitely grateful to you."

"All right, I accept," I replied without hesitation. This was certainly a reason that could not be easily ignored.

"But I do have some questions," I added. "When will I be able to return to my current life? And when I'm in the shoes of Monique Lefruit, will I be able to remember my present identity?"

"Regarding your first question, the answer is that you'll be able to return when things, in one way or another, have worked themselves out."

"Well that tells me absolutely nothing."

"With regard to your second question, however, they haven't given me precise instructions, so I think I can leave the choice up to you."

"To me? Then I choose to be able to remember who I am now."

"As you wish. Best of luck to you."

"So I'm 'leaving' immediately?"

But I heard no reply, only the voice of Lorelai who, on her way back from the kitchen with the box of Hungarian cookies, was saying to me, "Look, my telephonic little sweetie pie, I brought you the last three cookies. And you say I never think about you ..." Suddenly everything went black and I - Monique - found myself lying on a Berlin sidewalk illuminated by a streetlamp in the pouring rain as a bus sped away into the night. The next moment I saw the handsome face of a young lieutenant leaning over me. He had a thin moustache and a worried expression on his face.

"Are you hurt, my dear?" he asked, helping me to my feet.

"No, I don't think so."

"I don't know how you were able to avoid

that tram. For a moment there I thought it had run you over."

"You underestimate my agility."

"If I could get my hands on that idiot of a driver …"

I couldn't help but smile at the thought that, in this life, it was Lorelai who was protecting me.

"Come on, I'll walk you home," he said.

I nodded, and the nice thing was that I knew exactly where I lived: in a little two-room mansard just a few streets ahead.

It was incredible: I was still myself, but at the same time I was also Monique Lefruit. I knew exactly what to say and do in this altered reality. We kissed and it didn't seem in the least bit strange because as Monique I loved this man and as myself I loved Lorelai, and I knew that he was she.

CHAPTER 5

Before entering Germany with false papers, I had been an assistant to Professor Dimitri Genuflinski, a brilliant Russian scientist who'd taken refuge in Paris at the time of the October Revolution. The great scholar had discovered a substance capable of completely reversing someone's natural character, transforming, for example, someone sad into someone cheerful, someone dull into the life of the party, a criminal into a saint, or a politician into a paragon of honesty. This was undoubtedly an important discovery, but the professor (as often happens with scientists) hadn't considered all the possible consequences. Indeed, just as the substance was capable of turning bad into good, it could also do the exact opposite. He was so immersed in his studies that it simply had not occurred to him. In any case, when war broke out, it was immediately clear that his invention could be used to modify the nature of that mad German *par excellence*: Adolf Hitler. I had been chosen to take on the risky enterprise for three reasons: first because I was Professor Genufl-inski's assistant, second because I could think on my feet, and third because I spoke German even better than I spoke French.

The biggest problem was that the only way to administer this substance was for it to be absorbed through the skin's pores, like a sponge immersed in water or a croissant dipped in cappuccino. In short, it had to be dissolved in hot water in a bathtub and then the chosen subject had to take a dip. Now, given that the subject in question was Hitler, it was going to be a challenge. And yet, incredibly, it seemed at a certain point as if everything was coming together to ensure the success of our daring endeavor. But let's go back to the start.

Before leaving for Germany, Gert had been pointed out to me, if only for artistic merits, as a possible contact in order to get close to the *Führer* since he was part of his personal entourage. In point of fact, he was Hitler's official portrait artist. Having inexplicably promoted Gert to lieutenant despite there being nothing soldierly about him, the German dictator kept him close at hand for the sole purpose of painting multiple portraits of him in pompous triumphal poses. Gert was at his wits' end and was looking for a way out, but for the moment he was condemned to suffer in silence. He hated Hitler as much I did. I realized that as soon as I met him, in a bar one evening where he was sitting alone at a small table in front of a large mug of beer. He was doodling on a piece of paper and the results really caught my attention, for they were nearly all caricatures of the dictator in the most ridiculous poses: on top of a rocking horse, sitting on a chamber pot, hugging a giant sausage, and so on and so forth. When he realized I was observing him from behind, he nearly had a heart-attack for fear that I was an SS spy, but I immediately reassured him, then sat down at his table and asked him, "Are you a soldier or an artist?"

"An artist by vocation, a soldier against my will" was his reply.

We looked into each other's eyes and it was love at first sight. And so my assignment to get close to him, which for me was supposed to have been strictly business, ended up being a real pleasure. We had a wonderful evening. I felt I could trust him, so I told him who I was and he promised to help me. After a few days, in fact, he was able to get me hired by the company in charge of janitorial duties at Hitler's headquarters, thus allowing me free access every other day to that den of lunacy.

I'd already been working there for a couple of months when I had an unexpected stroke of luck. My boss, Inga, a walrus of a women with a typically granitic Teutonic disposition, informed me, "Erika (that was my false name), starting the day after tomorrow, you will prepare the baths for our beloved *Führer*."

I couldn't believe my ears. I hadn't been this

lucky since the day I'd won a crank-operated potato peeler at a county fair.

Inga explained to me that every other day before going to bed, Hitler took a hot bath, during which time he played with his rubber ducks and battle ships while wearing a Viking helmet and listening to Wagner on the record player. She warned me that the water temperature had to be exactly 37° Celsius, and that if I erred by even a single tenth of a degree, I'd share the fate of the other attendants who'd preceded me. I decided not to ask what had happened to them - I immediately went out and bought a good thermometer so as not to make any mistakes.

And it was at that point, the very night before the fateful day, just when everything seemed to be taken care of, every obstacle removed and smooth sailing ahead, that I was run over by a tram and died instantly. It was an outrage! Could you be any more unlucky? I had gone out to dinner with Gert to celebrate and on the way back destiny had played this nasty trick on me! Right then and there I was livid and protested vigorously, but no one paid any attention to me. All I could do was resign myself to wait for my next existence.

But now Justice was finally served and I had a second chance. Moreover, I found myself in absolutely unprecedented circumstances. For if only a select few people are aware of their past lives, I don't think there's anyone at all who's familiar with their next life. And not only was I familiar with it, I came directly from it. Gert walked me back home and came inside. We didn't make love because we were both a bit nervous, partly because of the near-accident and partly because of what the next day held. Before leaving (he had to go back to headquarters every night) he stayed to talk for a while. I sat on his lap and we gazed out the window over the rain-slicked rooftops of Berlin.

"It would have been terrible if something had happened to you, lemon pie, tonight of all nights." Even as a man, Lorelai couldn't help calling me these soppy names, though as a woman I found them a little easier to swallow.

"You mean" I asked him, "that if something happened to me the day after tomorrow, there'd be no problem?"

"Don't be silly, you know what I mean."

"Yeah, I know," I said, standing up and clenching my fists as I stared out into space. "Tomorrow's the big day. We finally get rid of the rotten apple, crush the cockroach, pull the decayed tooth, annihilate and vaporize once and for all this horrible nightmare that for too long has infected the entire world!" I'd gotten a bit carried away, and it was obvious that I'd yet to take the meditation and self-control classes that would have so much influence on my personality in my future life.

Gert tried to calm me down, saying, "We're not going to crush or annihilate anyone. With your little powder, what we're going to do is to perform a miracle and transform evil into good." Then he had me drink some chamomile tea, took me in his arms, brought me to bed, tucked me in and gave me a kiss, saying, "Now try to relax, dear. Tomorrow's going to be a long day."

CHAPTER 6

In truth the day wasn't very long at all, and before I knew it evening had come, that fateful moment when I was to prepare the bath for that detestable tyrant with the Chaplin mustache. Since it was my first time doing this, Inga stayed on to supervise. This I hadn't foreseen; with her there it would be difficult to secretly dissolve the powder into the water. I wondered if it might not be more prudent to wait until the next time, but I was too impatient to carry out my mission and decided not to postpone.

My nerves got the better of me, however, and I made one mistake after another. I even had to fill the bathtub twice because the first time I'd switched the numbers around, heating the water to 73° instead of 37°. When Inga put her hand in to check, she let out a shriek not unlike the warrior call of Wagner's Valkyries. Cursing and yelling that she'd have me sent in front of a firing squad, she left in search of a soothing balm and ordered me to get everything in order because Hitler was about to arrive.

Well, at least I was alone and could finally proceed undisturbed. I dried off the floor, emptied the tub and filled it up again, this time to 37°, lined up the rubber ducks and battleships, prepared the sponge and the violet-scented bubble bath, and, finally, took from my pocket the little tube of "magic" powder that would turn this wolf into a lamb. I was getting ready to pour it in the water when the *Führer* walked in, wearing nothing but his underwear. This was doubly shocking: first, because I'd been discovered, and second, because the sight of Hitler in his underwear was enough to make your stomach turn. With unexpected agility he pounced on me, yelling like a man possessed, "Betrayal! Attack! Guards!"

Two brawny SS officers came in and grabbed hold of me. I was trapped. Hitler, still in his underwear, was cackling in front of me, holding in his hand the little tube of powder that could have changed the destiny of the world.

"So, cutie," he said to me with the face of a self-satisfied pig, "you wanted to poison me, did you?"

That fool thought I'd wanted to kill him. It occurred to me that if we had been in my next life, at this point I would most certainly have morphed into the hairy, sharp-toothed monster Grunz and taken care of everything in the blink of an eye, but such thoughts were of no help at present. The situation seemed hopeless.

"Oh come on, what are you talking about?" I tried to rebut. "They're only scented salts."

Hitler sniffed the little tube and said, "I think not, I think not. As you should know, we members of the pure Aryan race have a highly-developed sense of smell and these, which you call scented salts, don't smell of anything at all." Given that I was under no illusion as to what was in store for me, I took the opportunity to reply. "Actually, I thought dogs were the ones that had a highly-developed sense of smell. Are you sure you're a member of the Aryan race and not a poodle?"

Hitler was furious. "A poodle! Me, the envoy of Odin, the holder of Thor's hammer, Bhal's saw, and Zhot's leveller? Me, the great initiate of the sacred lodge of Uhrl, the sect of Fwog and the confraternity of Hort? Me, the Grand Knight of Puk, minister of Nort, son of Uhdògg?"

"Well, that last one certainly seems appropriate," I commented, and seeing as I had the chance, I gave him a kick in the shin.

Now the little man with the ridiculous mustache really went berserk, cursing wildly as he hopped around on one leg. Then, with another well-placed kick, I got him in the other shin, at which point he literally began to howl.

This was understandably scant consolation for someone who a few minutes before had nurtured the hope of transforming the howling wolf into a bleating lamb, but you had to take what you could get. Hitler glared at me with fire in his eyes, then ordered his thugs to hold my mouth open and forced me to ingest the entire little tube of powder - thinking it was poison.

That madman! The powder had to be absorbed through the skin, not swallowed! At this point no one could predict what would happen. My throat burned and I put my hands around my neck, then my legs gave way and I fell to me knees. Convinced he'd poisoned me, Hitler and his guards started laughing scornfully.

I couldn't believe it. I might as well have been run over by that bus. In fact, I would much rather have taken my last breath in Gert's arms than hearing the cackling of those three hyenas.

Then all of a sudden, the warmth in my throat permeated the rest of my body. In the space of a few seconds my body was transformed, covering itself with hair and growing in size. My teeth turned into enormous fangs and my fingernails became long sharp claws. For some reason, Hitler and his guards stopped laughing. Then, in an instant, they and the rest of the Nazi higher-ups on the premises found themselves in the great hereafter, called to account for their misdeeds. It was as if their headquarters had suddenly been slammed by a tornado, sparing no one. No one except Gert, that is. I slung him over my shoulder, set fire to what was left of the building and jumped down from a window on the third floor. The flag with the swastika was still flying as the building went down in flames.

As I galloped away with strides a hundred meters long, it occurred to me that this was perhaps the remote origin of my future ability to turn into the monster Grunz. When I turned and saw Gert's slightly alarmed expression, I told him, "Don't worry. It's me, Monique."

He smiled tentatively, but he didn't seem re-assured.

CHAPTER 7

When we reached the open countryside, I stopped and lowered Gert down from my shoulders. I explained to him what had happened and he asked me, "Is that really you, honey? I can't believe it. What big claws you have, and what big teeth you have!"

"Sure, the better to eat you with. Give it a rest, okay? You aren't Little Red Riding Hood and I'm definitely not your grandmother."

"But are you going to stay like this forever?"

"What do I know ... I hope not. Anyway it's better that we disappear for a while. I wouldn't want people to get scared and a mob to come after us with pitchforks. We'll stay hidden until I'm back to normal and things have calmed down a bit."

I slung Gert back over my shoulders and set off at a gallop towards the south. I had decided to go to the Black Forest where I thought we would be safe.

I ran for several days until we reached our destination. We made our way through woods so thick that it was no mystery why it was called the Black Forest. I'd been darting between the trees for roughly an hour when, because of a miscalculation, Gert took a tremendous blow to the head from a low-hanging branch. I was unaware that it had happened, but shortly thereafter I felt him hanging limply down my back so I stopped and laid him down on a pile of leaves.

Half-conscious, he raved, "Sweetie pie, I'm going up to the library in the tower to look for a book on fruit tarts ... Where did you put that little pouch of gold coins we found yesterday in the basement?"

Incredible! Gert "remembered" things from his next life, meaning from when he would be Lorelai! Having been transported back in time just like me, he too must have conserved some traces of his future existence.

Since he was taking a while to regain his senses, I decided to take advantage of this extra time to prepare a surprise for him. I still hoped to reassume my normal appearance, but as long as I had the vigorous body of a yeti, it was foolish not to exploit it.

Close by I found a clearing where in no time at all, thanks to my newfound strength and speed, I constructed a cozy log cabin complete with a stone fireplace and flowers in the windows. Then I took Gert in my arms and brought him inside, laying him on the bed. He was still raving. From out of nowhere he exclaimed, "For all the unfurled foresails, cursed boatswain! Where's that barrel of rum we picked up in a Maracaibo?"

I wondered which past life he was reliving now. One thing was certain: his head had taken quite a blow.

Since I still had some time to kill, I took some money from Gert's wallet (I had none) and raced back down the road we'd already taken until I emerged from the forest and came across a farm. I quietly approached the house and left a sufficient amount of money on the front doorstep, then put a cow under one arm, a huge sack of seeds under the other, grabbed a coop full of hens with each hand and took off.

When I got home at dusk, Gert still wasn't showing any signs of improvement- in fact he was now running a high fever. He continued to rant, conjuring up episodes of lives lived at the time of the ancient Egyptians, the ancient Romans, King Arthur, and the Three Musketeers, so I hurried outside to build a fence, a stable, a barn, and a henhouse. When I returned, Gert's fever had broken and he was finally sleeping peacefully. Overcome by exhaustion, I too fell into a deep sleep and both of us slept for over sixteen hours.

The next day brought two pieces of good news: Gert was feeling better, though he still had a lump on his head the size and shape of an onion, and I was back to my normal self. No longer the powerful and monstrous creature of the previous evening, I was Monique once more. We celebrated by dancing gleefully in front of the house and this made me think of Lorelai, able to dance even as she simultaneously whipped up a couple of eggs *à la coque*. After all, it was still her whom I held in my arms, though I have to say that she's lighter on her feet and more graceful in her female version.

A truly extraordinary period began for us that day. Thanks to everything I'd found and built in my last few hours as a monster, we had everything we needed to live on our own. And that place was the answer to our deepest desires. We lived completely surrounded by nature, kind of like Tarzan and Jane. Cheetah was missing, but we didn't really notice. And if in the beginning we only planned on staying there for a short time, we ended up staying for thirty years. Time seemed to stand still, especially because, for some strange reason, we didn't age. After all those years, in fact, we were exactly the same as the first day we'd arrived and we didn't have the slightest clue why.

Our life proceeded calmly and peacefully. I took care of the garden while Gert looked after the animals, and I must say that we were both pretty good at it. I was able to crossbreed several types of plants to produce fruits and vegetables that were odd to say the least: beans as big as potatoes, tomatoes as big as water melons, watermelons as big as tomatoes, zucchini in bunches like bananas, cherry-flavored apples and strawberry-flavored pears. For his part, Gert rightly avoided conducting strange experiments on the animals, but he was able to increase their numbers and variety significantly. After only three years we had three cows, one bull, twenty-four hens, three roosters, six sheep, three goats, a cat, a dog and a giraffe. I never quite understood how or why we got the giraffe, but I couldn't argue with Gert when he pointed out how pretty it was.

In time we also learned about the properties of the many roots and herbs that grew naturally in the Black Forest by experimenting on ourselves. And in this field we made some very interesting discoveries. Besides the herbs and roots that were useful against headaches, stomach cramps and things like that, we found others with quasi-miraculous powers. For example, one allowed you to understand the languages of animals, one transformed you into a butterfly, another into a lizard, another made you forget everything, and yet another made you remember everything.

Generally, no one ever penetrated so deep into the Black Forest as to reach our clearing. Only once, a man dressed in gray with a folder under his arm materialized in front of us as if from out of nowhere. We were curious, given that we hadn't seen a living soul in years, so we welcomed him with open arms, only to discover that he was a fiscal agent who intended to make us pay years of back taxes and never-ending fines for having constructed without the proper permits. That time, the herb that made you forget everything came in really handy. We offered him a cup of tea made from it and sent him back where he'd come from. Then we drank the tea that turned you into a butterfly and went off fluttering from flower to flower in order to forget that unpleasant incident.

CHAPTER 8

But one day things changed. It was certainly foolish of us to expect otherwise, as if anything could last forever in a world in which everything is in continual flux. But I have to admit that the fact that we weren't ageing had led me, if only for a moment, to believe in the impossible.

One morning upon waking, we discovered that the forest had been enveloped in a very thick fog. Despite the fact that Gert advised me against it, I made up my mind to go outside and in the space of five minutes, I was completely lost. I tried to turn back but I could no longer find my way home. There was nothing but gray wherever I looked. I was able to stop myself from panicking, having fortunately retained some of the teachings of self-control that I'd receive in my next life from Master Astrakan Trazòff. I wandered around blindly for a while, trying to recognize by touch some tree or stone that was familiar to me, but with no luck. Fearing that I would stray too far, I decided to sit down on top of a large stone and wait for the fog to clear. I was going to be there for a while. I did some relaxation and concentration exercises that I'd learned from the aforementioned Master Trazòff. After about fifteen minutes, I was amazed to see the shadow of an ancient Germanic warrior - a massive figure made entirely of fog - emerge from the haze and approach with lengthy strides. But he hardly turned to look at me as he continued on his way. I was still recovering from my stupor when I saw an 18th century carriage pass by pulled by four horses with two ladies inside and a coachman in the driver's seat, all of them made of the same "condensed" fog. Then came an old lady, a man and woman arguing, some children chasing after each other, a man on horseback, and several others - all dressed in outfits from the past. I even saw an old Rolls Royce Silver Ghost drive by, made of fog and with four people inside.

After thinking it over for a moment, I reasoned that with my mind sharpened by meditation exercises, the fog was allowing me to see the faint spirit forms that are always all around us, but which we are normally unable to see. In any case, they didn't seem to be interested in me in the slightest, probably because they didn't think I could see them.

Suddenly, one spirit came into my view that seemed particularly agitated. It was in the form of a young man dressed in 17th century garb. He was pacing nervously back and forth in front of me and scratching his head. Every now and then he'd glance at me furtively and two or three times he approached as if he wanted to speak to me, but always decided against it. So I decided to break the ice and asked him, "Hello, is anything wrong?"

He was so surprised that he almost jumped, exclaiming, "So it is true! You can see me! I thought so, but I wasn't sure."

"I see and hear you. Maybe it's because of this fog."

"This fog, this fog ..." he repeated, turning suddenly pensive and serious. "It's the same fog that surrounded my castle just before she and her wolves arrived."

As he said nothing else, I was obliged to ask him, "She who? What wolves?"

"Who? She, she! She and no other! Who else?"

He was clearly too upset to give me a sensible answer, so I told him, "If you don't want to tell me, that's fine," and turned away.

After a few moments of silence he made up his mind to talk. "Her name is Volkjlla and she's the queen of the wolves. She always has a dozen of them by her side. She's beautiful. Her skin is as white as a moonbeam, her hair is smooth, long and black as night, and her eyes glow in the darkness."

As he was describing her, his tone of voice became almost ecstatic, but then it suddenly changed drastically and he exclaimed with alarm, "In truth, that woman is a demon! You must stop her!"

"Me?"

"Tell me, is there a strong, young and good-looking man nearby?"

"Yes, I'd say there is. There's Gert, my companion."

"So that's who she's come for!"

"Come for?"

"Let me explain. Every three hundred years Volkjlla sets out to steal a man's heart, at the beginning only in a figurative sense by making the poor man fall in love with her, but in the end she literally eats his heart. I know this all too well because I was her last victim. She came to my castle in Thurso, Scotland roughly three hundred years ago. Her wolves devoured all the inhabitants and I fell hopelessly in love with her. Don't blame me for this - no man she chooses for a mate can resist her."

"I could," I thought, but then I remembered that in this life I was a woman. I was still a bit confused.

"We lived together for three hundred years without ever aging," he continued, "thanks to an herb she put in our food, an herb that I thought grew only around my castle, but which I've seen here in this forest as well."

Finally the mystery of our eternal youth was revealed!

"They were three hundred marvelous years,

years of indescribable pleasures and delights, but at the end of this incredible time, on the last evening during dinner, she told me straight out that she had no choice but to kill me and eat my heart. It's quite an unpleasant thing to hear while you're adding a pinch of salt to your salad because it's a bit bland. Anyhow, I didn't even have time to reply because in the blink of an eye I had passed on into the great hereafter. Now do you understand why I said you have to stop her? You absolutely must if you don't want your companion to end up like me!"

The thing that irritated me, more than the idea the he might be killed and his heart devoured, were those three hundred years of indescribable pleasures and delights that Gert would have with wolf-woman, not to mention the fact that if he were going to spend the next three centuries in a Scottish castle, he'd miss his next rebirth as Lorelai and I would lose him in both this life and the next.

"Okay," I replied, "if everything you say is true, I agree that that woman has to be stopped. But what can I do?"

"On your own, not much. But you and your companion are not the only inhabitants of this forest. There is also a shaman who I believe can help you. I saw his house as I was wandering amidst the trees. It's about three kilometers from here towards the east. So, do you promise to try to stop Volkjlla?"

"Yes, I promise."

"I certainly hope you do."

"Well, I have already gotten rid of Hitler ..."

"Who is Hitler?"

"Oh, another lunatic leading a pack of wolves."

"Then you're the right person for the job. Now I can finally relax," he said, smiling for the first time just before he vanished into thin air, right before my eyes.

The fog was now clearing too, and this was good on the one hand but bad on the other, because if what the ghost had said was true, the fog's lifting meant that Volkjlla was gone and she'd taken Gert with her.

CHAPTER 9

Now that I didn't have to struggle through the troublesome fog, I easily found my way home and predictably, Gert was nowhere to be found.

And so it seemed that in both male and female versions, Gert (or Lorelai) was always getting himself (or herself) into situations that forced me to come to the rescue. It was obviously a constant factor in our relationship that would continue to crop up from one existence to the next.

I made up my mind to go see the shaman that the fog-shrouded spirit had told me about. After walking about three kilometers in the direction he'd indicated, I began looking for the shaman's house but I couldn't see it anywhere. I finally found it after a further hour of searching, and it was clear to me why neither Gert nor I had ever stumbled onto it during our exploratory wanderings. Hidden under plants and vines, it was perfectly camouflaged amidst the vegetation.

I knocked and the shaman came to the door.

He was completely different from what I'd expected: extremely elegant with a green velvet suit and a beige turtleneck sweater, well-groomed with combed-back hair, a moustache and a goatee, and a pair of glasses resting on his nose that were of the latest fashion. The first thing he said to me was, "Hello. Why did you knock instead of ringing the doorbell?"

It hadn't occurred to me to look for one, but upon closer examination, I saw that alongside the door was a doorbell complete with intercom.

"I didn't see it," I apologized, but he said that it didn't matter and showed me in. Inside I found not the laboratory crowded with cauldrons, decanters and alembics that I'd imagined, but a spacious living room with a fine carpet on the floor, a couch, armchairs, a radio, a record player, a television, a mini-bar, and even a nook with a piano.

"Please make yourself comfortable. My name is Popi, the shaman of the Black Forest. What brings you to my humble abode? Do you need some filter or potion to lift your spirits, to help you get back your *joie de vivre*? Or perhaps a little something to open your mind, to help you distinguish your friends from your enemies, or to give you access to ultra-sensitive realms? While you're thinking about it, I'll make you something to drink."

Well, how about that! I'd expected to meet a

scraggly old hermit with a long white beard dressed in rags, and instead I'd come upon a regular old dandy who wouldn't have been out of place in downtown London or Paris.

Popi took a bottle from the refrigerator and filled a cup for each of us with what I assumed was some kind of liqueur.

I was thirsty and gulped it down in one swallow, not noticing that he didn't follow suit. I (or was it "we?") had done it again! Once more I'd gone and trusted a stranger, though in this case he had come highly recommended by that guy made of fog from the 17th century. Well, it was no more than I deserved. Why would you ever trust anyone named "Popi?"

The room began to spin and everything in my mind became muddled. I saw myself first as a little girl playing "Scratch and Gouge" with my friends, then as I ran away from home to be an acrobat with the Potrì circus, and after as I turned into a monster and killed the *Führer*. Then, I began to have visions from my next life. The period spent in Transylvania as guest of the lovely Count Dracula, several adult-only scenes with Lorelai, and even the moment that I would rediscover the scarlet telephone and go back in time. In the end I completely lost consciousness, but not for long. In fact, I woke up after a few minutes and I didn't even have that typical post-hangover headache.

"Your story ... very interesting," said the shaman, smiling at me with his untouched cup still in his hand as he sat next to me on the couch.

"I hope you're not upset with me over this little trap I set for you. But you understand that I can't just trust any stranger who happens to walk by."

"Oh sure, no problem. I understand perfectly, and I hope you won't be upset at me for this," I replied, taking the cup from his hand and throwing its contents in his face. I got up and headed for the door, but he called after me, wiping his face with a handkerchief, "Wait, don't go. I can help you. Adam MacChicken was right."

I stopped in the doorway and, without turning around, asked, "And just who is Adam Mac-Chicken?"

"The ghost who sent you to me."

I was still angry, but I turned around and ... burst out laughing. The beverage I'd thrown in his face had had a truly bizarre effect. His nose had grown about ten centimeters longer, and so had his eyebrows, moustache and goatee.

It must be said that there's nothing better than a good laugh to get over being angry. He started laughing too and in the end I decided to stay.

I sat down next to him again. He said, "If you want to save Gert, you'll have to go all the way to the castle of Adam MacChicken near Thurso, in Scotland. That's where Volkjlla has taken him."

Then he stood up and invited me to follow him. "Come with me. I'll give you a couple of po-tions that you'll find most useful - if you know how to use them."

On the other side of the living room was a door hidden by a curtain. Going through it, we entered a vast room that actually resembled what I thought a shaman's house should look like. There were great bookcases full of ancient volumes, drapes on the walls bearing strange symbols, long tables cluttered with jugs, jars, long-necked bottles, alembics, pestles, test-tubes, and burners. On one shelf, a row of phi-als containing liquids of various colors was lined up. Popi picked two of them, one red and one yellow, and handed them to me. "Here you are. Drink these and you'll get the better of Volkjlla."

I took them and examined them closely, then commented, "I don't see any list of in-gredients. I have a rule about not ingesting anything unless I know what it's made of."

"You don't trust me because of that little trick before, right? But don't you realize how useful it was for me to really get to know you and to learn in mere moments exactly what it was that you needed? Don't you want to know what these two potions are for?"

"I'm listening."

"Each one has a permanent effect."

That didn't sound good. It was like saying there was no going back.

"In the past you turned into a monster, correct?"

"You know that perfectly well."

"Well, the red phial will give you back the ability to turn into that monster, whenever you like."

Here, then, was another characteristic that continued to accompany me through my various incarnations, despite some minor differences. For what I would be able to do in my next life only when provoked - turn into the hairy sharp-toothed monster Grunz – I would be able to do in this life at will, provided of course that the shaman was telling the truth and I had the courage to drink his brew.

Since it seemed like Popi was expecting some reaction from me, I said concisely, "Interesting."

"Just 'interesting?' You're not easily impressed, are you?"

"And what about the yellow one, what's that for?" I continued.

"Hmm. The yellow one is for gargling when you have a sore throat."

"What?" I exclaimed in amazement.

"What's the matter? Were you expecting something more spectacular? You should know that a good mouthwash is *very* 'interesting,' as you put it."

"All right, you win. I admit it, being able to turn into a monster at will is something fantastic and not merely interesting."

"That's more like it. You see, the proper re-cognition is not so much for me as it is for the plants from which these potions are extracted. If you don't give them the credit they deserve, you place serious limits on their powers and thus on the effects they will be able to achieve for you."

Despite my first impression of him, Popi was turning out to be quite the shaman. I decided I could trust him so I said, "Okay, that's true. Now tell me what the yellow one does."

"I already did. It's for gargling."

He began to laugh. "I'm joking. The yellow one is a very peculiar potion. It gives you the power to act through your shadow, that is, to detach it from yourself and send it out to do something. Or it can stay close to you and as-sist you as if it were another you."

I was tempted to continue joking with him and give him another "Interesting," but I couldn't help but exclaim, "Golly!"

CHAPTER 10

Now that Popi had gained my trust, the only thing left to do was to drink the two potions. I would have liked to ask him if there were any side effects, but I didn't want to drag things on any longer, so I uncorked the two phials and downed their contents in a single swallow. While the taste wasn't bad, there were a few side effects. I suddenly found myself suspended in space, at the feet of a man with an imposing build, a long green beard and a thick, tree-like crop of leaves on his head. He was seated on a throne carved out of a tree trunk whose roots disappeared into nothingness. This apparition said nothing to me but simply smiled, winking at me with the air of an accomplice. Then everything disappeared and I was once again in front of Popi the shaman who asked me, "Did you see King Florian?"

"Huh?"

"Never mind. Now let's verify immediately if the potions have taken effect."

"What do I have to do?"

"Clench your fists and flex all the muscles in your body."

When I did so, I immediately transformed into the great and powerful monster I'd been in the past.

"Holy smokes!" said Popi. "That is really scary! Now fill your lungs with air, hold it in for a moment, and then let it all out while simultaneously relaxing your muscles."

I followed his instructions and immediately turned back into Monique.

"Good, the red potion works very well," said Popi, satisfied. "But now let's go outside, because the yellow one can sometimes be problematic."

"What do you mean?" I asked worriedly.

"Oh, nothing too serious. The difficulty lies in the fact that a shadow by its very nature is used to doing the exact same thing that you do, so at first, when it's on its own, it can feel a little lost and be a bit clumsy. But after a few minutes, when it realizes its own incredible abilities, it gains confidence and becomes an excellent partner."

When we were in front of the house I asked, "What do I have to do?"

"The first thing you have to do is give your shadow a name."

"A name? Hmm, let me see. I think I'll call it ... Shadow."

"Okay. Now ask it to do something. Keep in mind that it can do anything, even what you consider to be impossible."

After thinking it over a moment, I said, "Shadow, you see that enormous boulder down there? Pick it up and move it behind the house."

I saw Popi go pale. My shadow detached itself from my feet and went over to the huge rock, lifted it up as if it were made of *papier--mâché*, and with a great leap jumped over the house and deposited it in the back. Finally, it returned to its place and reattached itself to my feet.

"Why did you make that face?" I asked the shaman.

"For all the nymphs in the woods! Didn't I just tell you that the shadow can be clumsy at first? We came outside specifically to prevent it from doing any damage, and you have it carry an enormous boulder over my house! Luckily your shadow found its legs right away, but I have to admit you made me sweat."

"Sorry, it didn't occur to me."

"All right, it doesn't matter. Remember - besides what you've just observed, your shadow has many other abilities that can be useful to you. It can take on any shape or form, it can divide, multiply, become as thin as a piece of paper, as small as an ant or as big as a mountain."

"Is there anything it *can't* do?"

"Let me think ... It can't talk, it can't fly, and it can't do anything where there's no light, that is to say, in the dark."

"With an ally like this and the ability to turn into a monster, rescuing Gert will be a walk in the park."

"Don't be too sure about that. It's never wise to underestimate your opponent. Good luck, Monique."

Popi extended his hand to say goodbye, but in this life I was a woman so I did what came naturally: I threw my arms around his neck and gave him a big kiss on the cheek to thank him, and this initiative of mine didn't seem to displease him one bit.

The time had come to leave, but something was bothering me and the shaman could see it in my eyes.

"What's worrying you? The long voyage?"

"No, it's not that. I'm concerned for my animals and the garden. Who's going to take care of them while I'm away?"

"Oh, if it's just that, then don't worry. I'll ask the forest elves to look after things. They'll be happy to."

That man sure was full of surprises. And to think that at the start I'd had my doubts about him! I said one more goodbye and then finally left. Returning home, I filled a backpack with some supplies, said goodbye to the cows, bull, hens, roosters, sheep, goats, cat, dog, and giraffe, got on my bicycle and started pedaling down the narrow path that snaked through the forest.

It was sad to leave these places where I'd spent so many happy years, but I had a mission to carry out: save Gert from a terrible fate. Poor Gert, condemned to three hundred years of indescribable pleasures and delights at the hands of that incredibly beautiful woman! Could there be anything more awful? Luckily for him I was racing to the rescue, equipped with the powers that the great Popi had bestowed upon me and determined not to allow such a terrible crime to be committed.

When it came right down to it, what did I really have to do? Just get to Scotland, find Adam MacChicken's castle, take on a hoard of ravenous wolves, and defeat their crazy, heart-devouring mistress. A cinch for the woman who'd killed Hitler.

As I was pedaling through the fields that lay beyond the forest, I thought about what the ghost of Adam MacChicken had told me, that no man was capable of resisting Volkjlla's charms. Yet I was more than convinced that if Gert really wanted to and, above all, if he thought about me, he could avoid falling under the spell of that wretched enchantress. The priority now was to get him back. Afterwards, however, he'd have a lot of explaining to do.

CHAPTER 11

It was incredible how much the world had changed in thirty years! Gert and I had been in the Black Forest for a good three decades, completely out of touch with the rest of the planet, and things had kept moving on without us.

One thing was certain: the world of 1973 was not the one I'd left in 1943. First of all there were a lot more cars, more colorful than before but, in my opinion, a lot uglier, with a few exceptions. There were also more houses. Everywhere enormous buildings had been or were being constructed, similar to giant bee-hives. And yet, at least at first glance, it didn't seem like people had turned into bees. But they sure did look different. Fashions had evolved incredibly. Clothes were much more colorful than before, many men wore their hair long and many women wore their skirts very short.

Even though all these changes piqued my curiosity, I nevertheless proceeded quickly on my way. I pedaled all day long as Monique, and then at night I doubled the distance covered during the day by pedaling for a couple of hours as the monster. During the day I didn't dare transform, fearful of being seen and taken for a yeti on holiday. Sometimes when I was in the open country and there was no one around, I'd let my shadow pedal for a little while, in which case I'd cover long distances in a short time.

One afternoon as I was going along a road in northern France, a Volkswagen van with flowers and strange shapes painted all over it pulled up alongside me. Four "hippies" were inside. I'd learned this word (which designated those youths with long hair and colorful clothing) by reading the titles of several magazines that were displayed outside a newsstand that I rode by. There were two guys and two girls, and they offered to give me a ride and stow my bike on top of their van. Since I was a bit tired, I gratefully accepted.

They really were quite the cast of characters. Their fascinating clothing consisted of flower-covered shirts, long skirts decorated with arabesques, and Asian-style earrings, necklaces, and rings. The inside of their van didn't disappoint either, with a Persian rug on the floor and Indian cushions on the seats.

"We're going to a rock festival near Arras," the driver told me. "Do you want to come?"

Until now I'd allowed myself no distractions,

but given that I'd already planned to stop for the night near Arras and I really liked these four, I agreed. We began to chat, and when I wasn't familiar with some of the rock musicians they mentioned, one of the girls asked me, "Where have you been hiding, in the middle of a forest?"

When I said "yes," their interest in me increased enormously and they asked me to tell them about my life. They seemed like open-minded people and I was curious to see how they'd react to my story, so I decided to tell them about everything that I'd been through. I thus recounted that I'd come from the future, that I'd killed Hitler, that I'd lived in the Black Forest for thirty years without ageing, and that I was now going to Scotland by bike to save Gert from the clutches of the wolf queen.

Their jaws dropped and then they began to laugh. I'd given them too much credit - they didn't believe a single word that I'd said. In fact, one of them asked me, "Yeah sure, and how many joints did you have to smoke to come up with that story?"

"Joints? What's a joint?" I asked, and at that point they really started laughing. If nothing else, you had to admit that they were a jovial bunch.

Since I did come from the future, I really should have known what they were talking about, but it sometimes happened that memories of my future life got overshadowed by those from my present life.

The response of one of the girls was to take out some small pieces of paper and, in the blink of an eye, prepare a long cigarette full of a green herb that didn't look anything like tobacco.

Then she lit it and, after taking a long puff, passed it to me. This gesture reminded me of the time in my future life when, during a trip to America, a redskin named Stampeding Buffalo offered to smoke a peace pipe with me. When I told him, "No thanks, I quit a long time ago," he got so angry that for a minute I feared for my scalp.

Not wanting to make the same mistake twice, I grabbed the joint and took a long puff. It's not that I really feared that those four good-timers would have scalped me if I'd refused, but honestly, why tempt fate?

Before it burned up, that lengthy joint had passed through the mouths (and lungs) of everyone until a quite sizeable cloud of smoke had formed inside the van.

The four good-natured youths were now laughing uncontrollably at whatever idiocy any one of them said, but I honestly didn't feel the least bit different. As I observed them with curiosity, I wondered why that stuff didn't have the same exhilarating effect on me. Then I became aware that a part of me certainly had been affected. My shadow was not only laughing just as hard as all the others, but it was also doing strange things like transforming into a poodle, a pig, a streetlamp, a seat, a cactus, and a turkey. It had completely lost its mind, and instead of obeying me, it was doing the first thing that popped into its head. Yet my fellow travelers were completely unaware of the show it was putting on, partly because they were too distracted by their own laughing and partly because they couldn't see through all the smoke, both in the van and in their heads.

I decided to open a window to let out a little bit of the haze but it was a careless move on my part because my shadow was sucked out along with the smoke.

I shouted, "Stop! Stop! It flew out the window!"

The driver slammed on the brakes and everyone turned to look at me. One of them asked me, "What flew out the window?"

I didn't feel like telling them it was my shadow because I knew they would think I was crazy. Looking out, I could see no trace of it. Where could it be?! Who would have thought that one stupid joint could deprive me of such a precious ally! What's more, I no longer had a shadow like everyone else, but truthfully this was the least of my worries.

"Oh, sorry, my mistake," I said, picking up an autographed photo of Janis Joplin off the floor. "I thought this photo of your friend had flown out the window, but wouldn't you know - here it is."

"Our friend?!" exclaimed one of the girls, and they all burst out laughing again.

CHAPTER 12

After all that commotion, the rest of the trip was calmer and more pleasant since the four hippies finally stopped cackling like hyenas and put on a tape of some really beautiful music. Little by little they all fell silent, as if deep in thought, and they didn't utter a single word until we reached our destination. All things considered, I liked them better that way.

"At this point," I thought to myself, "I could go to Hollywood and make a film entitled 'The Woman with No Shadow.' It could be a hit."

I sighed and consoled myself, thinking, "Well, at least I can still turn into a monster. Hopefully that'll be enough to save Gert."

We reached Arras at dusk, passed through the city as the first lights were going on, and soon came to the site where the festival was being held. It was an immense gated field with a few trees here and there. In the middle of it, an enormous stage had been set up for the musicians. I had never seen so many people together in one place. There were thousands of them, all very similar in appearance to my friends in the van.

I had decided not to stay for the concert, but rather to get back on my bike and continue pedaling northwards. I got out of the van and said goodbye, thanking them for the ride. But they wouldn't hear of it and forced me to come in with them. They told me they knew some of the organizers who would get us in for free. And shortly thereafter, we were all inside. As I've already said, there was a huge crowd and it was difficult for me to move in all that chaos because I'd insisted on taking my bike with me. So it wasn't long before I'd lost sight of the others and found myself all alone. I continued to move towards the stage, somehow making my way through that multitude of outlandish characters. Every once in a while someone offered me a joint, but I always declined because that first one had been more than enough. Finally I found a place to set up camp, right beneath a tree. It was a perfect location, and it had just become available because some guy, thinking that he was a pigeon or something like that, had fallen from one of the branches directly onto someone sitting below, and both of them had had to go receive medical attention. I leaned my bike against the tree and sat down on the ground in front of it, using my backpack as a pillow.

Soon after, the concert began. The first group was nothing special - not terrible, mind you, but nothing compared to the music I'd heard in the van. I decided to wait and see how the next one would be. If that too was disappointing, I'd give up the great spot I'd found and hit the road. In the meantime, this monster of a guy sitting next to me, half-buried beneath his hair and beard, offered me a piece of candy. I accepted and put it in my mouth, but it was not a piece of candy.

Why did I insist on being such an idiot? Was it possible I still didn't know where I was?

"Don't worry, sister," he told me, "it's strong stuff but it don't last long."

I felt like punching him in the face but I didn't have the time. The sky turned from black to red, and then yellow, green, lilac, spotted and so on and so forth, while the people and things around me began to appear distorted. Then everything disappeared and I suddenly found myself in my next life, seated on the checkered armchair in the blue parlor. Lorelai was on my lap, kissing the end of my nose and saying, "What a weird expression you have, sweetie pie. Has that Brussels sprouts dish I made given you a stomach ache? Wait here while I go get you a glass of unripe cucumber juice."

As I watched her leave, the armchair I'd been sitting in swallowed me up and I found myself once again in the shoes of Monique Lefruit in Nazi Germany. The SS had found me out and the firing squad was escorting me to my death. When we reached the place of execution, they put my back to the wall, aimed their rifles, and let loose. As soon as the bullets reached me, I was transformed into a white dove that flew up into the sky, while a voice was saying, "Don't be afraid. It's all an illusion. No one is born and no one dies."

Then it was suddenly all over. I was once again sitting against my backpack in front of my bicycle with a foolish expression on my face.

The guy who'd given me the piece of "candy" was no longer there, but now the music had started up again and this time, it was a real blast. The rhythm was so mesmerizing, in fact, that everyone had gotten up to dance. I thought I'd do the same and I was just getting to my feet when I saw everyone turn towards the stage and begin laughing and clapping their hands as if they'd just seen something both unexpected and exhilarating. I naturally wanted to see what it was but the people in front of me must have belonged to a race of giants. No matter how much I stretched, the only thing I saw was their backs. In the end I decided to climb the tree using my bike as a ladder, but once I was up there I saw something I wished I hadn't.

It was my shadow going crazy up on stage: dancing, shaking its hips, and jumping all over the place. Not only that, it was transforming in a thousand different ways, assuming mainly abstract shapes which broke apart and then came back together to the frenetic beat of the music.

Everyone thought that those "special effects" were part of the show, but I was the only one of the thousands of people present who knew what was really going on. I'd have given anything to be able to go up there and grab that rascal, but a sea of people were separating us and I had no hope of reaching it. The only thing I could do was to turn into the monster and get to the stage in a couple of leaps, but there was the risk of unleashing panic in the crowd with unpredictable consequences.

As I watched it perform, I wondered if my shadow would ever come to its senses and return to the fold. Maybe all this euphoria was the result of it finally gaining its freedom, emancipated from a long and hated servitude. Some people get left by their boyfriend, lover or husband – I, on the other hand, had been left by my shadow.

From my vantage point up in the tree, I saw it trip at a certain point and then fall down off the stage. "Serves it right for acting like lunatic," I thought. I know that you should never take pleasure in another's misfortunes, but when you feel as betrayed and abandoned as I did, it's difficult to think clearly.

Since my shadow was now a lost cause, I jumped down from the tree, took my bike and backpack and, making my way slowly through the crowd, headed towards the exit. Once outside the fence, I got back on my bike and started pedaling once more. When I got to open country, far from prying eyes, I turned into the monster and took off towards the north, as fast as a train shooting into the night.

CHAPTER 13

I resumed my normal appearance a little before dawn, just as I reached Calais. There were three hours to wait until the first ferry and I decided not to waste any more time, so I left the city, turned back into the monster, tied the bike over my shoulders, dove into the cold waters of the Channel and swam north towards the English coast. With only a few powerful strokes I was already in sight of the white cliffs of Dover, but I realized when I was a few hundred meters from the shore that there were people on the beach, perhaps fishermen or particularly early risers. It occurred to me that they might not take it too well if a fearful monster – for that's what I was – appeared on their shores, so before coming into view I resumed my customary appearance. In so doing, however, I forgot that I had the backpack and bicycle tied to my back. Their weight dragged me down to the bottom, thereby necessitating a quick change in strategy. I turned back into the monster, untied the bicycle, jumped on, and with my backpack strapped on, pedaled along the seafloor all the way onto the beach. I only returned to my normal appearance at the very moment I emerged from the waters, like a second Venus.

Now it's true that by shedding my monster form I was able to avoid people chasing after me with pitchforks. But I hadn't considered that seeing a young girl come out of the sea on a bicycle isn't exactly something you see every day. Everyone came rushing towards me, asking me who I was and where I'd come from. At that point I could have made up a whole series of plausible explanations: that I was a native to the area, that I was a scholar involved in a scientific experiment, that I was a biologist interested in mollusks or what have you. But nothing of the sort came to mind so I admitted to them candidly, "I came from Calais by bike." As I had already noted on other occasions, sometimes honesty is the best policy. Everyone started to laugh, saying, "And she expects us to believe her! Here's another one who just wants to get in the papers! Young people today! What will they think of next!"

In short, no one believed me and everyone went on about their business. Everyone, that is, except one. A well-dressed, portly, bald little man with a moustache had in fact stayed put and continued to watch me, smiling.

"I believe you," he said, "because I am just like you."

"What do you mean, sir?"

"I beg you, no 'sir' is necessary," he replied and extended his hand. "A pleasure to meet you. I'm Frederic Prock, and I'm an inventor like you."

"Like me?"

"But of course! Come now! Let us not deny our very nature! We are the avant-garde of humanity, the light of the world! You mustn't lose heart. I too am often derided by these imbeciles, incapable of recognizing genius even when it's standing right in front of them.

Come with me, I live only two hundred meters from here. You'll be able to dry your wet clothes and have a hot cup of tea. And in the meantime, if you wish, you can explain to me how you were able to breathe underwater and withstand the intense pressure and cold. Did you by chance use a transparent thermal film? A pressure compensator? An oxygen exchanger?"

The thought of having dry clothes and drinking hot tea was quite appealing. I decided to play along and accepted his invitation.

Frederic Prock really did live two hundred meters from there – two hundred meters straight up. His house was located on top of a white cliff that rose imposingly from the beach. To reach it you had to climb a steep staircase carved into the rock that was, obviously, two hundred meters long. To make matters worse,

I had to carry my bicycle without the benefit of being able to transform into the monster. Luckily, my inventor friend offered to carry my backpack. When I got to the top, my tongue hanging out of my mouth, I feared that he might have trouble believing that such a delicate young lady could have had the strength to cross the channel by bike, but fortunately his mind wasn't plagued by such doubts.

The stairway ended right beside his house which was very close to the edge of the cliff. It was quite small, but had a sort of hut next to it where Frederick probably constructed his inventions. One thing was certain - there was an incredible view from up there, both of the sea and down the entire coast.

We went inside and he immediately lit the furnace to help me dry off, then prepared the tea and handed me a cup. When he saw that I was reasonably warmed up, he asked me, "Did you see my furnace? What do you think it runs on – wood, coal or gas?"

He waited no more than half a second for my answer and then added, "None of the above. Try to open it."

"I can't see very well," I said, "there's too much light."

"What you are looking at is the world's very first air furnace, one of my humble inventions," he said with a satisfied little smile. "When it comes right down to it, extracting heat directly from the air, or more precisely, from the oxygen contained in the air, was the obvious solution to the problem. Any numskull could have figured it out. Well, I'm that numskull."

"That ... numskull?"

"It's just an expression. Now I'd like to show you a little something else I'm particularly proud of."

He stuck his hand in his jacket pocket and pulled out a little matchbox which he then shook so I could hear the sound. It seemed as if there were two or three pebbles inside. Then he looked at me with a smirk.

Since he wasn't forthcoming, I said, "Well?"

Without saying a word he ran outside to get a pot full of earth, placed it on the floor, and then proudly showed me the contents of the match box: an acorn and a large blue pill.

"Watch this," he said. He buried the acorn in the earth, placed the pill on top, and poured a glass of water over it. The pill dissolved completely into the earth, after which nothing else happened.

Seeing my perplexed expression, he explained, "This is the most potent fertilizer in the world, capable of bringing any plant to complete development in under a minute. Another one of my humble inventions."

I stared at him with my mouth agape, then asked him, "Do you mean that in less than a minute there'll be a fully grown oak tree in here? But there's not enough space! And there's not enough earth in that pot!"

He looked at me frantically and exclaimed, "Damnation! That hadn't occurred to me!"

Suddenly, a plant growing at an unimaginable speed shot up out of the pot while its roots, developing just as quickly, shattered the terracotta container into a thousand pieces. Within an instant, the trunk was enormous and had dozens of branches popping out in every direction. The roof of the house was thrust high into the air, breaking apart and taking parts of the walls down with it. The tree, now gigantic and no longer supported by its roots, leaned to one side and toppled over, flattening what little remained of the small house.

We didn't even have time to react. We were still sitting where we were moments before, me with my mouth open and the cup of tea in my hand and him wide-eyed. Only a miracle kept us from harm in the middle of that cataclysm.

"Quite an amazing discovery, at any rate," I commented. "Do you think just any old numskull could have come up with *this* invention?"

"No," Frederic replied, getting himself together, "this required a particularly talented numskull."

CHAPTER 14

I was feeling slightly guilty, given that Frederic had destroyed his house due to his enthusiasm to show me his discoveries.

"I'm sorry," I told him, patting him on the back, causing his jacket to release a small cloud of powdery debris. We were both covered in dust.

"Oh, that's okay," he replied. "It's not the first time I've brought my house crashing down. That's one of the reasons why people don't take me seriously. But I don't let these little setbacks get me down. It just means I'll have to sleep in my hut for a bit. I'll rebuild my house even better than before. In fact, it may well be the chance to test out another of my humble inventions: compressed-water bricks."

His irrepressible scientific spirit was truly admirable.

"But tell me about you," he continued, going back to our previous conversation as if nothing had happened. "Tell me how you were able to cross the Channel by bicycle. I have to admit that I'm very curious."

My brain immediately began to conjure up a thousand different stories in search of a plausible explanation, but in the end I decided that it would just be better to tell the truth. And this for two reasons: the first was that honesty, if possible, is always the best policy, and the second was that I considered Frederic to be too good of a scientist to be able to fool him with technical arguments.

Once again, honesty turned out to be the winning card. My inventor friend was fascinated to learn about aspects of reality that were completely unknown to him. Phenomena like receiving phone calls from celestial bureaucrats, traveling through time from one existence to another, transforming into terrifying monsters, losing one's shadow and squaring off against wolf-women weren't, until that moment, exactly part and parcel of the world he'd experienced.

"Incredible!" he exclaimed. "I've never heard anything like it. But as a scientist, I need proof. Before I can give credence to something, you know, I'm accustomed to running innumerable experiments, checks and counterchecks ..."

I didn't wait for him to finish since I already knew what he was getting at. Without saying a word I clenched my fists, flexed my muscles and instantly turned into the monster.

"By Jove, I believe you, I believe you!" he exclaimed, his eyes opening even wider than when the house had collapsed. When I returned to my normal appearance, he found the courage to add, "I hope my skepticism didn't offend you. My doubts were of a purely scientific nature."

"Yes, yes, I understand," I said. "But now I have to say goodbye. The time has come to jump back on my bike and start pedaling north once again. Thank you for the tea."

I got up but he stopped me, taking my hand. "Hold on a moment, I can't just let you leave like this. I'm profoundly in your debt. Thanks to you, my research will now have vaster horizons. Did you say you have to get to Scotland? Come with me, I may be able to help you."

Making his way through the debris without letting go of my hand, he headed towards the hut. I could only hope he wouldn't cause that structure to come crashing down around our heads too. But my fears were unfounded or, more to the point, misdirected. Rather than worry about the hut itself, I should have been concerned about the rocket that was inside it.

It was small in size, poised on its little launching pad as if ready for takeoff - but I noticed that its launch trajectory would take it right through the roof! Then again, having witnessed Mr. Prock's lack of concern for his own house, I presumed that he would consider that to be no more than an insignificant detail. Though the rocket was very nice-looking, all silvery with red and yellow lightning bolts painted on its sides, its pleasing appearance did nothing to alleviate my sense of alarm.

"So what's this?" I asked, immediately realizing that this wasn't a very intelligent question.

Frederic responded, "A potato peeler."

I corrected myself. "What I meant to ask is whether this is what you wanted to show me, or if there's something else."

"No, this is it," he said, with the same satisfied smile he'd had when he showed me his air furnace. "With this, you'll be in Scotland in only a few minutes."

Oh dear, my fears were justified - this rocket was meant for me.

It wasn't that I didn't think Frederic was a good inventor, but his last performance with the fast-growing oak tree had exposed his tendency to neglect potentially important details.

I would have been very irritated to end up unexpectedly on the moon or on Mars. I was, after all, on a mission: to save Gert from those three hundred years of indescribable pleasures and delights in the company of the wolf queen.

My inventor friend likely guessed what was going through my mind and tried to reassure me. "There's nothing to fear. This rocket is guided by a crossed-valve electronic brain, such that once you enter your destination co-ordinates, its margin of error is no greater than thirty meters."

Well, when he put it that way! If there were crossed valves, then we could all rest easy! What could possibly go wrong if there were crossed valves! I took my backpack and bicycle and headed towards the rocket with the same enthusiasm as Marie Antoinette must have approached the guillotine. My mistrust might have been slightly excessive, but you have to keep in mind that I'd only just miraculously survived the collapsing house.

"I'm sorry but there's no room for your bicycle on the rocket," Frederic said as he flipped through a large book that lay on a side table. "I'm afraid you'll have to leave it here."

"What are you looking for?" I asked him.

"The coordinates. In this book are the coordinates for the entire world. Where was it you said your boyfriend was? A castle in Scotland, right? I believe you said it was close to Thurso. Here it is! Perfect! I'll bring you down a couple of kilometers away so you'll have time to formulate a plan of attack. Now get in, close the door, sit down and put on your seatbelt. I'll take care of the rest."

We shook hands and he said to me, "Good luck. I've already entered the coordinates. As soon as you're ready, I'll begin the countdown."

I saw the roof of the hut open up as I climbed up the ladder, an encouraging sign, but after strapping myself into my seat, I began to wonder: "Why on earth am I blasting off in this rocket? After all, even if I arrive two or three days later it won't make a difference. I'll just get down and tell him."

So I unfastened the seatbelt, opened the door, and was halfway out when the missile took off without any warning, any noise, any flames, any smoke, anything at all - just fast and silent like an arrow launched into the sky. I certainly had underestimated the inventive genius of Frederic Prock.

CHAPTER 15

The rocket was accelerating at a dizzying speed and I was hanging out the still-open door, so I had no other choice than to turn into the monster. This was the only way I'd have the strength to hang on. However I soon realized that getting back into the cabin would be a whole other kettle of fish. The fierce winds held the cockpit door wide open and prevented me from getting close enough to scramble back inside. I decided to try hanging down from the open door like a gorilla from a tree branch, but all that accomplished was to tilt the rocket up and cause it to veer off course. If as a woman I didn't weigh much at all, especially since I'd always looked after my figure, as a monster I must have weighed a couple of tons. All that heavy swinging could lead to only three possible outcomes: my getting into the rocket, the door breaking clean off, or the rocket changing direction. I was naturally in favor of the first option, but fate chose the third one instead. I realized as much when I glimpsed the nose of the rocket slowly turning until it had totally re-versed its course. It passed back over Fre-deric's hut, recrossed the Channel, and was now heading steadily south. I would have liked to have let go at that point but I was too high up, and I had no desire to return to land only to be flattened like a pancake. When the rocket began its descent, to avoid sharing its fiery fate, I let go and curled up tightly in prepara-tion for impact. I hit the ground at great speed, rolling like an enormous bowling ball. There were even objects similar to bowling pins in my path, but instead of pins they were trees, well-anchored to the ground with their strong roots. The ecologist in me was over-joyed that I hadn't uprooted them, but I couldn't help thinking that if they had flown up into the air as good bowling pins normally do, I'd certainly have ended up with a few less bruises.

When I recovered from the blow and re-sumed my normal appearance, I realized with some dismay that there was another good reason to be happy that I hadn't knocked over those trees - they were all old acquaintances. In fact I knew every single one of them very well since the place I had come to rest was on the edge of the Black Forest.

It felt like playing one of those board games, when you land on the square that says "Go back to the start." But if there was one thing I'd learned from my next life, and brought back with me to this existence as Monique, it was that you should never lose hope. While most of us keep in our hearts the things we've learned in our past lives, I had the rare opportunity to make use of teachings that came from my next life! Upon further reflection, however, I remembered that the life I was now living and that was unfolding in the past relative to my next life actually constituted the future relative my future life, because it was really occurring after what I'd lived through before coming back to the past. Better, perhaps, not to get sidetracked by such quibbling.

I sat down on a rock and began to consider what to do. I could have found another bicycle and pedaled back the same way as before, but perhaps there was a better option. In the end, I decided to pay another visit to Popi, the shaman. He had helped me once; perhaps now he could help me again. I made my way into the forest along those trails I knew so well and in no time I was in front of his house, well-camouflaged amidst the vegetation. Rather than knocking, this time I rang the doorbell which played a couple of notes from Vivaldi's *Primavera*.

Elegant as always, Popi appeared at the door and exclaimed, "Well, what are you doing here? I thought you would be in Scotland," and then, glancing around here and there, he asked, "Where's your boyfriend? Don't tell me you weren't able to save him," and finally, looking at the ground beneath my feet, he asked, "And where's your shadow?"

"How about inviting me in?" was my response.

"But of course, excuse me. You took me by surprise, that's all. Make yourself comfortable and tell me everything."

We sat down in his spacious living room and he offered me a cup of tea. I refused, wary of what had occurred the last time I'd accepted one from him, and proceeded to tell him what had happened.

"It's my fault," he said finally. "I should have warned you that cannabis makes semi-detached shadows lose their minds. But you honestly didn't seem like someone who needed such advice."

"I usually don't do that sort of thing."

"I see, so you're a victim of circumstance. The guy who robbed the bank said the same thing."

"I didn't rob any bank," I replied, annoyed.

"Don't get me wrong, I'm a shaman and I'm used to using herbs of all kinds, but I use the right herbs at the right time and always for a purpose. This is very important."

"Listen, what's done is done, and after all, I can live perfectly well without a shadow."

"You might be able to live perfectly well without *it*, but *it* certainly won't be able to live for very long without you."

"What do you mean?"

"I mean that after turning into so many different things, your shadow will end up not being able to remember what its original form was and, at that point, it will disintegrate."

"No!"

"Oh yes, and the terrible thing is that we can do nothing more than hope it finds its way back home on its own. But come now - I don't think you rang my doorbell just to tell me about your adventures."

"Right you are. I wanted to ask if you could help me to get back to Scotland as quickly as possible."

"Did you ever think about taking an airplane? There are some excellent flights that could get you to Edinburgh in a couple of hours."

"Yes, I know," I said, slightly embarrassed, "but seeing as I was in the neighborhood, I was hoping that you ..."

"I'm only kidding – you did the right thing coming to see me. I just happen to have a syrup in the back, an extract from forest mushrooms, that's just what you need. Every time you take a spoonful of it, you can teleport to the destination of your choice.

"Perfect!" I exclaimed. "But why didn't you give that to me in the first place?"

"I wanted to make things more interesting for you. I thought it would be more satisfying to complete your mission without too much assistance. After all, I did give you the shadow and the ability to transform into a monster - that seemed enough. I didn't want to do *everything* myself!"

I stared at him for a few moments and then said, "You know, Popi, you sure are strange. You act like I enjoy going through all this non-sense."

"I know that you'd never admit it, but it's the truth. I know you better than you know yourself. Now come, let's go get that syrup."

CHAPTER 16

We went into the great back room I remembered from before. My friend the shaman had to get up on his tiptoes to reach the shelf where a row of particularly dusty phials was lined up, each one different from the next. He took one of them and used a rag to remove the layer of dust that was covering it, and then held it up to observe it against the light.

"It's been a long time since I've used this syrup. I don't get around as much as I used to. There's not much left but it's still good. As you can see, I always write the expiration date on my products."

I took the little bottle in my hand and read the label. It said: "Traveler's syrup. Expires April 2127."

"Yes, I see," I commented. "It's still good for some time."

"Yes ... time," said Popi, suddenly deep in thought. "There are times when it seems so short and we wish there were more of it, and there are times when it never seems to pass.

It has such a strong influence on us, and yet it doesn't exist."

"Huh?"

"Oh nothing, I was just thinking out loud."

"Okay. Well, goodbye then, I need to get going."

"Before you leave, don't you want to stay a while and catch your breath?"

"No, I've wasted too much time already. Who knows what Gert's doing with that woman at this very moment? Just thinking about it makes me boil."

"I knew someone else who was driven by the exact same emotion," said the shaman, smiling. "He was a moor in the service of the Venetian Republic, a certain Othello."

"You mean the guy from Shakespeare?"

Without responding, Popi poured the syrup onto a spoon, careful not to spill a single drop, and then said, "I'd give you the whole phial to take with you so that you could use it for the return trip as well, but as you can see there's nothing left."

"First let's worry about getting me there. We'll deal with getting back later."

"Excellent. Now say out loud where you want to go."

I gathered my thoughts and then declared, "To Scotland, two kilometers from the castle of Thurso."

"Well, my dear Monique, good luck and have a good trip," Popi said, putting the spoon into my mouth.

I was afraid that the syrup would have an unpleasant taste, especially since I'm not a big fan of mushrooms, but it was actually quite nice since it had a hint of raspberry. The last thing I saw was the shaman's smiling face and then everything broke into pieces, like a mosaic whose tesserae were suddenly taken apart and then recomposed into a completely different image.

I reached my destination in an instant but there was a slight problem - the place was not at all as I had imagined it. I'd expected to find myself in the middle of vast green pastures full of sheep, cows or horses, and instead I'd ended up in the middle of a dank and insalubrious swamp. Night was falling and, what's more, I was slowing sinking into quicksand.

It was a very unpleasant situation and I didn't see any way out. There was nothing near enough to grab on to, and the more I moved around, the quicker I sank. I tried turning into the monster but in this case it didn't help; in fact, the greater weight made me sink down even faster. I quickly changed back to my normal appearance.

If only I had a little more of Popi's syrup! But unfortunately there were no pills, no balms, no syrup, just the feeling that my time had come at last.

Although I'd long since learned that death didn't really exist, at least not in the sense of a complete and utter cancellation of self, I was still annoyed that my heroic enterprise should come to an end in this stupid little bog.

Then, suddenly, something happened. With the slime already up to my throat, I became aware that my legs had gained greater freedom of movement, as if they had popped out beneath the mud and were now just hanging in empty space. Then I felt two strong hands grab me by the ankles and pull me down with a jerk. I rocketed through the layer of mud and found myself sitting on the solid floor of a cavern underneath the swamp. It was poorly lit. When my eyes adjusted to the half-light, I could make out a strange creature looking at me with curiosity. He was holding a small torch whose flame emitted a dim light.

Though he was completely covered in fur and filthy with dirt, I could tell that he was a man. He had very small, almost nonexistent eyes and his face, or should I say his snout, was pointed. He had short legs and long, strong arms with thick nails at the end of his fingers. I asked myself what he was but my mind was unable to find an answer. My intuition, however, promptly suggested: "It's obvious. He's a mole-man!"

It's remarkable how easily intuition can find answers to questions that baffle the rational mind. I truly hope that the latter will one day gain access to the wisdom that currently eludes it.

So there I stood in front of a mole-man. Okay, but just what is a mole-man? I didn't have to wait long for an answer. "Pleasure to meet you, my name is John Holedig and I live for the most part underground. I love digging long tunnels and eating tubers and roots. You were very lucky that I happened to be passing by under here or you'd have come to quite an unpleasant end. Quicksand can be merciless to those who venture into it carelessly."

"The pleasure is all mine," I replied, getting to my feet and extending my hand, which he nearly crushed in a handshake that felt like a vise.

"I used to be an ethologist," he explained to me, "and during my study of moles I was bitten by one of these curious and amusing little creatures. From that very moment I began to change, gradually acquiring their habits and even their appearance. One day I made my kitchen collapse by digging a tunnel underneath it, so my wife threw me out."

"Oh, I'm sorry to hear that," I commented.

"Ultimately I think it's been good for me. Now I can live my underground life to the fullest and dig shafts and tunnels to my heart's content."

I'd never heard a story quite like this, and if I hadn't heard it firsthand from the mole-man himself, I probably wouldn't have believed it.

"But how did you end up in this swamp?" he asked me, so I proceeded to tell him all about my adventures. When I'd finished he began to laugh like a maniac. "And I thought my story seemed strange!" he exclaimed as soon as he'd caught his breath.

Then, turning serious again, he added, "You really were lucky to meet me because the castle of Thurso can only be reached via my tunnels. Getting there above ground is practically impossible because it's surrounded by a great ring of swamps. Volkjlla's wolves stand guard there day and night."

"You forget that I can transform into a monster."

"I don't know what type of monster you can turn into, but I don't think it can compete with three thousand ferocious wolves."

Three thousand ferocious wolves? Gosh, maybe I really had underestimated my adversary.

"With my tunnels, however," the mole-man explained to me, "we can come up directly under the castle, inside the dungeons, and thus avoid both the swamps and the wolves."

All of a sudden I realized that I was starting to become pretty fond of moles!

CHAPTER 17

With him in front and me behind, we set out by flickering torch light through a network of seemingly endless tunnels. Every now and then the route would fork or even branch off in three or four different directions. At these junctures John Holedig would stop to reflect for a moment, then choose one of the tunnels and set off quickly down the path. I'm not sure how long we went on like this, because although we were only a couple of kilometers away from the castle, it was also true that the tunnels almost never went in a straight line, but rather zig-zagged here and there. At a certain point we found the tunnel obstructed by a large square stone. The mole-man turned towards me and whispered, "Here we are. Behind this large stone are the castle dungeons. Now we have to be very quiet."

Then with a show of great strength, he pushed the rock forward with his long strong arms. We emerged into the dungeons which at first glance seemed deserted. Nevertheless my friend seemed worried and looked around nervously. Finally he whispered, "The first time I came here I didn't know where I'd ended up. And if I had known, I would never have come. When it dawned on me, I nearly fainted. I immediately turned around, put the rock back in place and left, promising myself never to return. I've only come back to escort you, but now it's goodbye, best of luck, and I'll be seeing you."

He handed me his torch saying, "You'll need this more than I do. I can see perfectly well in the dark even without one." Then he smiled at me and disappeared down the tunnel, pulling the camouflaging rock back into place behind him.

I was grateful to him for his precious help and also for not shaking my hand again, since it was still hurting from his initial salutation.

I decided to transform right away into the monster since I expected to have some pretty nasty encounters down there. I clenched my fists and flexed my muscles, but nothing happened, and I remained the slight and rather puny Monique. For a moment I was panic-stricken. I was surrounded by thousands of ferocious beasts, inside and outside the castle, all of whom were just waiting for a naïve, helpless young girl to pay them a visit. I tried two or three more times to transform but it was no use. What's more, I couldn't even go back where I'd come from because, as Monique, I wasn't strong enough to move the huge rock blocking the entrance to the tunnel. What a situation! This time I was really done for! All I could do at this point was to go forward and search for a way out of the trap I'd gotten myself into.

Like all respectable dungeons, these were cold, dark and damp. There were many cells, some closed off by small thick doors and others by bars. Yet it seemed that they were all empty. I wandered around for a while, going down one long narrow corridor after another, until I suddenly heard someone calling me: "Monique! Monique! Is that really you?"

My heart jumped into my throat because the voice seemed very familiar. I approached the cell where the voice had come from, put the torch up to the bars and saw a man - but was it Gert? It was hard to say because although it sure looked like him, he was now much fatter, nearly twice his previous size.

It stands to reason that if someone gets locked up in a dungeon, even if they're not there for very long, they should at least look a little worse for wear - not as fat and round as a watermelon. This was the thought that stopped me from rejoicing and leaping into his arms, the bars notwithstanding.

But his words melted my last remaining doubts like snow under a hot sun. "Monique, buttercup! How did you manage to find me? After a whole year, I'd lost all hope of ever seeing you again!"

Only Gert could call me buttercup or sugar pie or names like that, a habit he would not only carry forward but increase in his next existence as Lorelai. I lunged towards the bars, barely avoiding smashing my teeth against them, and embraced him as best I could, exclaiming, "Oh, my dear. I've finally found you!"

But there was something in what he'd said that didn't make sense, and I felt the need to bring it to his attention. "What do you mean, *after a whole year*? Only a few days have passed since you disappeared from home."

"You see, doodle bug, there are many things you don't know," he replied.

"And you do?"

"Yes, and once I tell you, everything will be clear."

It always irritated me when he beat around the bush and acted mysteriously, but I was too happy to see him again to lose my temper.

"All right, so tell me. I'm all ears. But first we need to get you out of here."

"That's simple, sugar pie. The key is right there behind you, hanging on the wall."

I turned around and saw that there was indeed a large key hanging on a nail.

"This is one of Volkjlla's sadistic tricks," said Gert as I grabbed it, "putting the key right in front of my face but just out of reach. I tried everything I could think of to reach it, but to no avail."

I opened the bars and was finally able to embrace him properly. In doing so I realized just how fat he had become, but decided it was not the appropriate time to broach the subject.

After all the customary effusions that are routine on such occasions, Gert began his story by inviting me to sit down next to him on the wooden table that probably served as his uncomfortable pallet. "You should know that until about ten years ago, Volkjlla wasn't the queen of the wolves."

"You don't say? And what was she?"

"She was a completely normal woman, at least as far as her appearance went."

"Wait a second," I interrupted him. "First tell me how you know all this."

"Because I read her diary."

"Volkjlla keeps a diary?"

"It's one of the few habits she's kept up after her transformation."

"What transformation?"

"Hers. As I was saying, Volkjlla was originally a normal woman, or almost, until she found an old treatise on 'lesser magic' on a used book cart. 'Lesser' means that the powers you can obtain by studying that book are, fortunately, limited. Essentially it taught two things: how to subjugate one and only one animal species, and how to gain unlimited powers but only within a circumscribed area, for example a forest, a mountain, a house or a castle. Now if Volkjlla had been normal, she would have chosen to acquire dominion over, let's say, doves or dogs or horses, putting together a magnificent show that would have earned her fame and fortune. But she chose wolves, and I also know why."

"Why?"

"She wanted to take revenge on all men after her ex-fiancé, Teodolindo, abandoned her at the altar on their wedding day, fleeing to the cry of 'Freedom! Freedom!'"

"So it's all Teodolindo's fault."

"Maybe, though I think the poor guy had some good reasons for taking off. Anyhow, that's why Volkjlla chose wolves. And what's more, she's also turned out to be a terrible queen."

"How's that?"

"Because she's enslaved them, making them even more ferocious and aggressive than they were before. They obey her because they're forced to, but in truth they hate her."

After taking a moment to digest all these revelations, I asked, "And what can you tell me about her magical powers?"

"Volkjlla's powers are unlimited, but only within the walls of this castle."

"So that's why I wasn't able to transform!"

"Transform?"

"And she'll certainly know that I'm here!"

"You can count on that, sweetheart," Volkjlla said, materializing from out of nowhere. She stood outside the cell and locked us in with three turns of the key.

"It would seem, dear Gert, that it is not your destiny to spend your last night alone. Tomorrow morning both of you are going to have a nice walk outside the castle. My friends the wolves will give you the warmest of welcomes. I've told them and they're already licking their chops."

Having said this, she burst into laughter and left. All in all, it was a very melodramatic scene that I was sure I'd seen before in some film or perhaps in a cartoon but, in real life, I have to say it made quite an impression.

CHAPTER 18

Once we were alone again and seeing as we had the time, I told Gert all about the adventures that had brought me to this point, leaving him nothing short of amazed. Then I asked him to finish his story since there were still a few things I didn't understand. Indeed, I'd expected to find him at Volkjlla's side and absolutely smitten with her, certainly not shut away in a cold dark cell in the castle dungeon.

"I'll start from my kidnapping," Gert began. "I was at home peeling some potatoes when I saw Volkjlla appear in front of me. She ordered me to follow her and, given that she was surrounded by a pack of unfriendly looking wolves, it didn't seem wise to object. As soon as we were out of the forest, I was hit over the head with what I think was a stick and lost consciousness. When I came to, I was already here in the castle in Volkjlla's bedroom and she was wearing a long sheer, 'Now-you-see-me, now-you-don't' sort of nightgown."

"'Now you see what?" I asked.

"What do you mean, 'what'? It was the 'now-you-see-me, now-you-don't' sort. Isn't that clear enough?"

"Okay, okay! Go on."

"She was beautiful."

"Okay, okay! Go on."

"Hold your horses, just let me tell it."

"Who's stopping you?" I was starting to get irritated.

"Anyway, she was convinced that I ..."

"That you? That you what?"

"Can you please calm down?"

"Me? I'm perfectly calm."

"Good. Anyway, she was convinced that I'd fall like a slave at her feet."

"That would really stink."

"What would?"

"Her feet."

I wasn't making much sense because my nerves were beginning to get the better of me. My head felt like it was on fire. I'm not sure why, but Popi's seemingly random allusion to Othello came to mind.

"Well, do you want to know?" Gert finally burst out. "I never fell at her feet!"

"Oh really, then where did you fall?"

"Nowhere. Don't you get it, Monique? She thought she could overwhelm any man with her magic, but with me she failed!"

"But how?" I asked with a foolish-looking smile as my head began to cool down.

"I've thought if over for a while, and I've

come to the conclusion that maybe all the other men she'd brought here weren't really in love with other women, or maybe not as much as I am. Her magic had never had to compete with true love, and she was no match for it."

Oh my gosh! That was so romantic! The kiss I gave him was no less passionate than those that Lorelai would give me in our next life. He'd certainly earned it!

"Volkjlla refused to accept defeat," he went on, "and kept me prisoner in her room for three days and three nights, continually trying to win me over with more and more extreme forms of seduction, but in the end she was forced to surrender. She was livid and she locked me up down here, feeding me hyper-caloric foods to fatten me up before feeding me to her wolves. Did you notice that I've put on a little weight?"

I was tempted to minimize and say, "Well, just a little," but since I'm firmly convinced that a healthy relationship should be based on honesty, and I was also slightly annoyed by those "more and more extreme forms of seduction" that Gert mentioned, I exclaimed, "Of course I noticed! You look like a damn hippopotamus! But don't you worry! As soon as we get out of here, I'll put you on strict diet and you'll be back to your old self in no time."

"Thanks for your optimism, Monique, but I don't see much hope for us on the horizon. Even if you're able to turn into the monster once we're outside the castle, I don't think you'll have a chance against all those ferocious wolves."

"Never say never, Gert. But tell me one thing. Since you've read that harpy's diary, did you discover anything that her magic depends on that we could destroy? A talisman, her book ..."

"To undo her power over the wolves, we'd have to destroy her book of magic, but she keeps it well-hidden somewhere. As for her magical powers, it's a little bit more complicated ..."

"How so?"

"When Volkjlla chose the castle as the place to work her magic, it became completely saturated with it; so in order to destroy her powers, we'll have to lay waste to the castle."

It seemed that at that point there was little left to say. Knocking down the castle was out of the question as its solid rock walls were a couple of meters thick at least. For a while we said nothing. Then I broke the silence: "But you haven't answered my question."

"Which question?"

"I asked you to explain to me why you said you've been here for a year when you've only been here a few days."

"Oh, that. It's simple. Time passes differently here in the castle. While outside only a few days have gone by, in here a year has passed."

After thinking it over for a moment, I said, "Then what Adam MacChicken's ghost told me in the Black Forest, that Volkjlla kidnaps a man every three hundred years to devour his heart ..."

"Exactly. In reality, three hundred years in here correspond to no more than two or three years on the outside."

"Now I understand. And she has a different fate in store for you because you refused her?"

"Yes. She hates me so much, I think she's afraid my heart will give her indigestion."

CHAPTER 19

Waiting for daybreak in a castle dungeon is no easy task because, well, you have absolutely no idea what time of day it is. Despite the fact that our situation was not exactly rosy, we were nonetheless able to get some sleep. Being together again was a great source of comfort.

Morning was heralded by the arrival of the guards, eight of them to be exact, well-armed and ferocious looking. Gert explained to me that they were actually wolves transformed into men, just like all the other soldiers and servants we would meet within the bounds of the castle.

They led us directly into the outer courtyard and brought us to a halt in front of an enormous gate, beyond which hordes of wolves were waiting to greet us. "Strange," said Gert, looking around, "I thought Volkjlla would come to savor her victory."

"Victory is only sweet when it's hard-fought," said the wolf-woman, appearing before us from out of nowhere. "But with you there was no need to fight. Never have I had such insignificant adversaries. Nevertheless, I'll enjoy the festivities my wolves have in store for you from up in the tower."

Now that I saw her for the first time in broad daylight, I had to admit that she really was very beautiful, as beautiful as she was evil and hateful. I needed to do something to get under her skin, to spoil her party. I got up on my tiptoes, took Gert's face in my hands, gave him a long kiss on the mouth, and then turned to face her, smiling. For a second her cheeks flushed, but she immediately regained her composure. Saying nothing, she averted her gaze and lifting up off the ground. She flew to the top of one of the towers that rose on either side of the large gate that had just opened up in front of us. We were pushed outside, finding ourselves on the drawbridge that spanned the large moat that encircled the castle. Roughly twenty meters away, the wolves awaited us. I had never seen so many of them in one place, and I wondered why the ones in the back had bothered to come at all. There would certainly be nothing left for them from the slim pickings of Gert and myself.

I tried to transform but the drawbridge was apparently part of the castle and thus still under Volkjlla's power. As soon as I'd crossed it, however, I mutated and told Gert, "Stay behind me!"

I'm not sure if the monster's size and strength were automatically adjusted according to the size and strength of its foes, but what I did know was that I had never felt so much energy rushing through my body. Though the wolves were confused by my transformation, that alone was not enough to change the odds in our impending clash, still undoubtedly in their favor. Yet something had changed. The wolves in front were no longer destined to have more to eat; rather they were in line to get more of a beating. I turned and looked up towards Volkjlla. She seemed rather amused up in the tower. In fact from her vantage point, the disparity between the two sides on the field was clear to see. No matter how powerful I was, what could I do against that sea of ferocious beasts except maybe live to fight a little longer?

Though the wolves continued to hesitate, it was clear that the situation was coming to a head, so I decided to make the first move. I was about to lunge at the nearest beasts when I heard the sound of a car horn honking wildly in the distance. I looked up and Gert peered out from behind me, and what we saw was a powerful black car with a sort of rostrum attached to the front, plowing through the wolves and tossing them helter-skelter as it went.

"See that?" I said to Gert. "Help is finally here!"

"But who is it?"

"I don't have the slightest clue."

But when the car came closer, maneuvering between us and the ravenous hordes, I recognized it immediately. How could I *not* have recognized it, given that it was a part of me that had found its way home like a second prodigal son? It was my shadow, all right, and it had come at exactly the right time. This idea of the car was really excellent, but given that I was back in control of it now, I exclaimed, "Quick, Shadow, form an insurmountable barrier between us and those horrible beasts!"

It promptly obeyed, turning itself into a wall that was high, black and – naturally – insurmountable, putting us out of the reach of those thousands of hungry beasts once and for all. With the defensive phase now concluded, it was time to attack. Not the wolves, mind you- they were themselves the victims of Volkjlla. Her evil had to be destroyed at the root. "Shadow," I said, "split in two and have one part of you go look for Volkjlla's book of magic."

A black panther broke away from one end of the long protective wall and raced inside the castle. Before the wolf-woman up in the tower had time to react, the shadow was back with the book of magic between its teeth. It turned it over to me and I held it up, showing it to Volkjlla.

"Well, what do we have here?" I yelled up at

her. "Recognize this?"

The wolf-woman was frozen with rage, glaring at me with eyes that could spit flames. But there was nothing she could do as we were now outside her castle. These two adversaries of hers, so insignificant only a few minutes before, were now on the verge of destroying her power.

My shadow was still beside me in the form of a panther so I tossed it the book, saying, "Shadow, tear it to shreds!"

It only took a moment and there was nothing left of the book of magic but a pile of tiny scraps of paper that a gust of wind blew into the air.

Gert embraced me and said, "You have one amazing shadow."

I don't think there are many women who have received a compliment like that from their partner.

But there was still one thing left to do, so I ordered, "Shadow, turn into a demolition crane and raze that castle to the ground!"

An enormous black ball attached to a chain began to swing back and forth, slamming into the strong stone walls until they crumbled and fell. I was sorry to destroy this splendid manor that had stalwartly braved the passing of the centuries but unfortunately it had had the bad luck of being infested - not by mice or ghosts like an ordinary castle, but by the terrible Volkjlla.

With the loss of all her magical powers, Volkjlla reverted to her normal appearance, the one she had had before turning into wolf-woman. In fact when the dust from the castle's destruction had cleared, we saw a disheveled, dust-covered little woman roaming through the ruins and mumbling, "What happened to my pretty little castle? ... And my book of magic? ... Rats, I really need to go to the hairdresser's ... and then to the laundromat ... Just look at this mess ... I need to call the cleaning lady."

It was time to hit the road so I said, "Shadow, put yourself together and turn back into the car you were before."

"What about all those wolves?" Gert asked worriedly.

"Now that they're free they'll divide into packs and go back to where they originally came from."

"Not that, I mean are they going to attack us without the wall?"

"Not if we get into the car right away and close the doors nice and tight."

Once we were inside, we watched the wolves approach the car, circle it, and then head slowly and threateningly towards Volkjlla.

"Don't you think, rosebud," asked Gert, "that we should save her and take her with us?"

"Take her with us? That doesn't seem like a good idea, and besides, I wouldn't want to deny the wolves what's rightfully theirs. Shadow, step on the gas and get us out of here."

Our big black car took off at full throttle in the midst of all those wolves, tossing them helter skelter just as it had when it arrived.

CHAPTER 20

As we travelled south through the English countryside, seated comfortably in the back of our custom-built vehicle, Gert asked me, "Listen, sugar plum, can you explain to me why, if your shadow could turn into a car, you pedaled so far by bike on the way here?"

"It's very simple. It didn't occur to me."

"What?"

"You heard me. I didn't think of it."

Gert looked at me amazed and then began to laugh, but what I'd told him was the absolute truth. I explained that in the beginning I had considered asking my shadow to turn itself into an airplane, but when the shaman told me that it couldn't fly, I'd hastily concluded that I would have to deal with transportation on my own, forgetting that there were other means of transport. But this was no longer of any importance because everything had worked out in the end and now we were returning home, to the Black Forest.

We arrived in London towards evening and

were fascinated by that metropolis, so full of light and life. It was the early Seventies and London was full of long-haired youths with multi-colored oriental-style or flowered clothing and colored uniforms. This psychedelic floral style wasn't only in clothing but could be found just about anywhere you looked: in murals on the walls, in store windows, in furnishings ...

There was also music everywhere, most of it simply marvelous.

After all of our recent misadventures, we really just wanted to enjoy ourselves and we were sure this was the right place to do so. When we reached Piccadilly Circus, we got out of the car and I said to my shadow, after thanking it of course, that we had no further need of it at the moment and that it could take a rest. Unexpectedly, it gave me kiss on the cheek, a sign that it too was happy to have found me again, and lay down on the ground reattaching itself to my feet. Once again I projected a shadow again just like everyone else. It might seem unimportant but, as so often happens, you only learn the true value of something when you lose it.

After escaping so many dangers, it seemed incredible that Gert and I were together again there in London. There was a feeling of lightness as if we'd both just been freed from a heavy burden. We held hands and it seemed like we were walking ten centimeters above the ground. The city was ours alone.

We stepped down off the sidewalk and were both run over by one of those characteristic red double-decker London buses. We both died on impact and I suddenly found myself back in the yellow parlor, sitting at the large walnut table where I'd left the scarlet telephone. Lorelai was next to me, offering me the box of Hungarian cookies and saying, "Listen, my befuddled little sweetie pie, do you want these cookies or not? I'm not going to stand here all day!"

I thanked her, took a cookie, and began nibbling on it. Lorelai sat down next to me, biting into one of the cookies she said she'd brought for me. "So," she asked, "is this telephone permanently on strike? It doesn't want to ring anymore? Have you tried plugging it in? Oh right, there is no plug. Maybe that's why it doesn't work. Don't you think we should give it one? It certainly looks nice and all, but if it doesn't work ..."

How she was able to say all this, eat the cookie, and not choke remains a mystery.

"The telephone works perfectly well," I answered. "I just spoke with some guy."

"Which guy?!" she exclaimed, her big blue eyes opening wide. "When did you speak with him? While I was away? Damn, you could've called me!"

"I didn't have the time. I was sent back into the past to settle some unfinished business in a past life and, wouldn't you know it, you were there too ... as a man."

Lorelai knew me too well to think that I was pulling her leg, and she began to protest. "Damn, so it was something that had to do with me as well. This telephone is so mean! Why does it have to play favorites? I don't understand why it decided to exclude me."

Then her expression changed and, looking resolute, she exclaimed, "Now we'll see who's boss." She picked up the receiver to give a piece of her mind to I'm not sure whom, but as soon as she'd put it to her ear, she froze with her mouth agape. Someone was speaking to her and she began to reply, practically in monosyllables. "Yeah, sure ... Okay ... Apology accepted ... What's that? ... It's the least you can do ... Better late than never ... All right."

She hung up and immediately disappeared right before my eyes, then reappeared a moment later.

Seeing as she didn't say anything, but just sat there bewildered with a blank stare on her face, I asked her, "What happened? Who was on the phone?"

She looked at me, smiled, and said to me, "You know what?"

"No, what?"

"We both really need to be more careful when we cross the street."

The Scarlet Telephone